The Perfect Stranger

The Perfect Stranger

Dennis Danvers

SPEAKING VOLUMES, LLC
NAPLES, FLORIDA
2020

The Perfect Stranger

Cover design by Hannah Linder

ISBN 978-1-64540-272-5

For Nell
1880-1957

The novelist is the perfect stranger, the fellow who sits down beside you on some journey or other, and draws you into his world of words where he does the most marvelous things to you. You might fly. He might enslave you. He'll almost certainly fuck you, convert you, something intense. Laws don't matter, even those of the so-called universe, for one brief ride, a 1000 pages at most. And then, here's the best part, you part from the stranger with the world outside the journey unchanged. All the changes are within, where the perfect stranger lives.

—Gene Sanders Wilkerson, Thoughts on the Novel

So long as you write what you wish to write, that is all that matters; and whether it matters for ages or only for hours, nobody can say. But to sacrifice a hair of the head of your vision, a shade of its colour, in deference to some Headmaster with a silver pot in his hand or to some professor with a measuring-rod up his sleeve, is the most abject treachery, and the sacrifice of wealth and chastity which used to be said to be the greatest of human disasters, a mere flea-bite in comparison.

—Virginia Woolf, A Room of One's Own

Chapter One

Discovery

Thar She Blows!

Our souls are like those orphans whose unwedded mothers die in bearing them: the secret of our paternity lies in their grave, and we must there to learn it.

—Herman Melville, Moby Dick

Genevieve spots it with her headlamp—a lone box smaller than the rest, nested in the far corner of the attic under a frosting of undisturbed dust as if the house had formed around it. She puts on her gloves. She's already wearing a mask. The box is heavyish. Nothing rattles or shifts. She slides it to the top of the stairs where there's more head room, sucks it clean with the minivac, and sees it's a box that originally held five reams of paper. She hefts it. It doesn't feel full. Scrawled on the lid in Wilkerson's characteristic loopy hand are strings of letters—TMS, SPH, SSD, a couple of others obscured by packing tape—that mean nothing to her. She feels a chill.

She almost missed it. She's been up here several times without spotting it. Like it didn't want to be found. It might be a box of blank pages, or they might not be blank. She isn't supposed to open sealed boxes and mess with the artifacts, but she's too curious, and the tape across the lid has failed in the heat of the attic and flaps loose at the ends. A tug will free it. She sits down cross-legged and slides the box between her knees, strips the tape. She removes the lid.

Holy shit.

She stares at it in the beam of her headlamp for the longest time, trying to imagine how it could be real, perfectly flat, undisturbed, unseen for more than a decade: The title page of a novel by Gene Sanders Wilkerson, whose attic this once was—called *Scapegoat Phoenix*—a novel she's never heard of. She's been the graduate research assistant for Dr. Bent Morely, the leading Wilkerson scholar in the world, for going on three years now while she works on her dissertation—and if Wilkerson wrote a thank-you note to his great aunt Florence in Jersey for that swell middle school graduation gift, it's likely Genevieve has laid eyes on it and catalogued it.

She's adored Wilkerson's work much longer than that, so when his mountain retreat was donated to the university a few years ago by his surviving brother, Tom, as a way of getting out from under the back taxes, she jumped at the chance to inventory the remaining items— mostly useless junk—just to be where he wrote all but the first of his great novels. Wilkerson despised his family and made sure they never made a dime from his work, safely ensconced in his literary estate. He once described his work to an interviewer as "one long attempt to flee the vicious, vacuous tedium of my roots."

Genevieve can relate.

The house had been a mostly empty hulk, badly in need of repair when Tom unloaded it. She's grown used to its quirks and creaks and loves being here. She's alone in the house, tucked into a mountain hollow, acres of wilderness in all directions. She loves driving out here from the city like Wilkerson used to do, eventually selling his house in town when his last wife died, and living here alone until his death from a sudden heart attack in the meadow outside. She winces imagining it. He lay there for days before he was found Genevieve often takes her lunch on the porch where he wrote when weather allowed, looks off into the mountain valley, and tries to imagine what it would've been like to be him. She used to think she couldn't stand the solitude, though the more time she spends out here, as the weeks and months and years go by, the more she wonders if that's true. These days, when she's in the city, she thinks about being here. With Sandy.

Supposedly, Wilkerson quit writing novels the last decade of his life, electing instead, like Thomas Hardy, to return to poetry, essays, and short stories. The eight published novels she's read and reread countless times are all there are, and all there were ever going to be. She's never quite forgiven him for abandoning the novel.

The poetry sucks, the essays are windy and sentimental, and the short stories are weird and quirky, which isn't a particularly bad thing, but since many regard Genevieve as weird and quirky and more than a little fucked up, she prefers to resist expectations and take her art straight ahead and down the middle. Genevieve once tabulated the frequency of keywords in *Wilkerson Studies*, the journal she assists Morely in editing—meaning she does everything, and he takes all the credit—and wasn't surprised to discover *nostalgia* topped the list. *Melancholy* was a strong contender. *Epiphany* goes without saying.

A Wilkerson novel always puts her where she wants to be. She imagines herself and Sandy to be kindred spirits across time, like soul mates. Sandy was Wilkerson's nickname among his closest friends and all but one of his five wives, the shrill one who called him "Wilkie"—a name (and wife) Genevieve abhors. She would've preferred to be kindred spirits in a nice big bed or a mountain meadow. Nobody writes the al fresco fuck like Wilkerson.

She's studied all the photographs of his several wives and lovers and concluded she's his type, that he would definitely go for her—a big-eyed, leggy nerdy intellectual who adores his work and likes sex and enjoys long walks in the woods. If only he hadn't died at sixty when she was thirteen, a year before she first read his novels from the library at fourteen, no idea he was dead. She started with *Don't,* his controversial YA novel (his third published), and read them all, not knowing he was dead, that there would be no more, not realizing that the photos under cellophane on the library copy jackets were from a long time ago, one taken on the porch downstairs, the wind blowing in his hair—he always had the beautiful hair, blonde, then white. The trees behind him are bigger now. One is gone altogether, blasted by lightning. She learned about the world through those novels. Or rather, they were the lens through which she viewed everything. The real world was a dull and shabby place. Sandy showed her otherwise.

She finally works up her nerve to look inside the box and examine the contents, to touch his untouched pages. There are five novels in all, apparently complete, with Wilkerson's characteristic The End at the close of each with the date and place he completed it. All here, all written between 1995 and 2005, the so-called Silent Years. In addition to *Scapegoat Phoenix* are *The Mad Statue, Willingly, A Sandstorm of Destinies*, and *Missing Persons.*

She takes out her phone, forgetting you can't get a signal on this side of the mountain, then starts to head for the car but thinks, why should I call Morely and watch them become *his* great discovery? Deathly afraid of spiders—she's slaughtered a few at his behest when they show up in the office—he never would have ventured into the dark corner under the eaves where she found these manuscripts. The definitive bibliography published last month has her name buried so deep even her mother couldn't find it if she bothered to look, when in point of fact, Genevieve did it all—everything but write the dedication to Bent's *beloved wife,* whom he refers to with much greater frequency when she's not present as *stupid cow*—for a pittance, for a nice letter someday to a search committee chaired by some pal of his at a backwater state college somewhere offering the slow grind to tenure. It's not like he's even a nice guy. Truth is, Bent's a dick.

She stares at the box. No one expected to find anything like this, not here, not anywhere. Supposedly everything of any value was hauled away by little brother Tom years ago. Tellingly, he left behind all the memorabilia from his big brother's successful writing career. Maybe Tom never made it up into the attic, cluttered mostly with abandoned camping gear and broken lamps Genevieve catalogued and hauled away over a year ago. Tom's arthritic and half blind and thought his brother was an asshole and called his novels stupid. Maybe he didn't think five undiscovered novels would be worth anything. The thought makes Genevieve burst out laughing.

She's feeling a little high, jazzed, like some gorgeous man is hitting on her. Five gorgeous men. She can't take her eyes off them. Five undiscovered novels. She remembers the hysteria on NPR last spring over some newly discovered short story by Carver. Or maybe it was Chandler. Genevieve isn't so much into short stories. You can't get lost in short stories. She imagines her story, however, on NPR, echoing from the walls of her shower—Genevieve Slidell, Brilliant Young Graduate Student Makes Literary History! She manages to get lost in *that*.

Out of the hiss and steam of this imagined shower steals another thought like a phantom in the mist:

She could have them all to herself. They could be her discovery, her five discoveries. It would be easy to find them elsewhere, somewhere that isn't university property and she isn't on the clock. She quickly thinks of several places more likely to have stumbled upon them, and how she might arrange such a fortuitous accident now. She takes the speed of her thoughts to be a sign of true inspiration. Her scalp is tingling, her heart racing. Besides, whatever else she does, she *has* to read them. Now.

To think a thing is to do it in the region of the world that matters most, since it has the final say about the rest—your mind—a favorite Wilkerson theme. To disown your imagination, the gateway to your soul, is to disown yourself. Once the unthinkable has been thought, it must be done! Anything else will eventually silence your soul. As you can imagine, characters who think like this have no trouble keeping the pages turning even as you're wondering why anyone would be so incredibly reckless, at the same time Wilkerson persuades you it must be so! The brother's right. They are a bit stupid, but that's part of their charm. They speak to our inner Fool. At least that's what she claims in the introduction to her dissertation. She even plays the Tarot card. Wilkerson was a fan. That's how he met the shrill wife. She read his cards at a party, which proved to be a winning seduction ploy. Sandy was on the rebound and vulnerable. Genevieve learned her junior year: If you can smuggle the Tarot into a critique, you're never at a loss for something to say. Wilkerson's five wives are a favorite distraction as well, but Genevieve generally shuns the subject in her work. Not because it's beneath her, but because in her heart of hearts she sees them as rivals who took unfair advantage of Sandy's unfulfilled longing for Genevieve.

She figures the reason Sandy wasn't happy with all those other women was because she's his soul mate, and she wasn't born yet. She hasn't really worked on this theory since she was fifteen, so don't press her for details, but it was incredibly sustaining back then, and she's never quite let it go.

***

In a true act of Wilkersonian bravado, Genevieve soon finds herself driving back to the city with five novels in her trunk, the windows all rolled down, destiny whipping through her hair, giddy with freedom. Inspired: Conspiring with the blue sky and flaming fall foliage to imagine the apotheosis of Genevieve Slidell, the tall skinny kid with her hand up who's run out of classrooms, more glad to learn than teach, who'd secretly rather be a character in a novel than analyze or teach one.

The typical Wilkerson novel picks up the tale of a vagabond down on his or her (usually her) luck who comes upon a crisis, a crossroads, compelling eyes across a cafe table, a pang of old regret—*something* that sets them on a clear course for the rest of the novel where they meet other vagabonds on similar trajectories. Young, old, men, women. Disillusioned idealists cut loose from their moorings, seeking, always seeking, who in the end, for a while at least, find something of value. They're polyerotic, and there's lots of sex, sweet disillusioned idealist sex, that not only gets you hot but has you thinking about it after—the nuanced dialogue, the meaning of a touch. No one is silent in a Wilkerson bed. Genevieve likes words. They reassure. Eyes are good, but too scary if they're silent. If someone's peering into your soul, you deserve a little feedback. As for touch, that's what it's all about, isn't it?

Wilkerson liked to travel. One theory for his having quit writing novels is that he grew to hate flying so much, he couldn't stand to do the travel required to research his novels. Genevieve over the years has vacationed almost exclusively in the Wilkerson locales she could only intensely imagine as an adolescent, rereading the novels on windswept moors, in rain forests, and in squalid little hotels down by the docks. She sat in the same restaurant and ordered the exact same meal Camille in *The Forest of Forgetfulness* orders before boarding the train to Barcelona, but Genevieve had to imagine her own handsome Spaniard to fuck in transit, who, naturally, looked a lot like Sandy.

In Chiapas, she fucked her real *guia* on top of a pyramid under the full moon. That was a high point, or maybe it was a low, something a

Wilkersonian heroine might do, though the sex would've been better, and she did have a little too much trouble shaking the guy loose when it was time to move on—ended up climbing out the bathroom window to catch a midnight bus out of Ocosingo, leaving her copy of *Without Regret* on the bedside table. *No es recomendable.* She should've known he was a little weird when he told her he was a *brujo*, a witch, instead of finding it sexy.

In one of her early masturbatory sex fantasies, she imagined she was Winona Ryder doing it with Edward Scissorhands, Mom's massive kitchen shears, cold and hard, balanced between her young breasts. When she heaved with pleasure, the shears clattered to the floor, and she was discovered by Mom. That was a turning point for her and Mom. Good or bad, it's still hard to say. Mom can smother with openness, and Mom is wide open when it's her turn. It's a bit overwhelming, and like everything with Mom, lopsided.

Fortunately, Genevieve's moved on from Scissorhands. She's had a thing for writers since she's been here in Richmond as a doctoral student, where there's a steady stream in the MFA Creative Writing program. She finds them interesting and intense, but mostly she's drawn to them because she's always wanted to be one, and maybe if she gets close enough, they'll let the secret slip. So far, she has nothing to report, but at least you don't have to climb out the bathroom window. She's had some seriously pissed-off poetry dedicated to her at readings when there was no way out of the room except through the floor, but that's just added to the Legend of Genevieve. She aspires to be the sort of person of whom it is said, *What is her story?* (Place the emphasis where you like, let it roam through various states of delight and exasperation.) But she knows her rep is actually Morely's Drudge, the Wilkerson freak.

Everybody thinks she fucks Bent, but he's not about to shit where he works, as Mom would say—Genevieve too, when she's home in

Texas. Things are more genteel here in Richmond. Genevieve doesn't do genteel. Genevieve's essential to the Legend of Bent—Brilliant Hard-Working Charmer. Only one-third of that's true. Genevieve and her predecessors have labored long and hard to create the illusion of the other two-thirds. Genevieve has many fine qualities. She's the first to admit charm isn't one of them. The man's a walking argument against tenure. Bent tells her she's the best assistant he's ever had. Gosh Bent, thanks.

Genevieve looks into the rearview, imagining the five novels inside the trunk. Where are they set? Who goes there? What will she discover? The *brujo* on the pyramid told Genevieve she would be blessed by the gods with an incredible gift and awesome responsibilities, which she kind of doubted at the time since she hadn't come yet and he was already talking about her future and putting on his pants, but maybe *this* is what he was talking about: Five undiscovered novels, a gift from the fucking gods if ever there was one.

We make destiny by living, myths by remembering is one of her favorite Wilkerson lines. She has a ten-year-old t-shirt with that on it, so thin you can read through it. She's twenty-seven, approaching the end of her most recent three-year plan—work for Bent until the money runs out. He's been talking about keeping her on, finding additional funding, giving her more time to finish the dissertation. She envisions this generous offer as a long coil of rope with which to hang herself. Such talk makes her panicky inside. She's been looking forward to wrapping up the dissertation and moving *on*. Enough genteel. Enough Bent's girl. That's what the sweet Professor Emeritus who occasionally shuffles up and down the halls called her the other day. *You're Bent's girl, aren't you? You've been at it for a while now. He always snares the brightest ones somehow.*

Her destiny has shown up just in time.

***

She stops at Food Lion for supplies. Pizzas, muffins, coffee, chips, salsa, red wine in a box. She has a lot of reading to do. She texts Bent to tell him she has horrible cramps and heavy flow. Too much information should keep him away indefinitely. It's her way of letting him know that even though he likes to fuck breathless twenty-year-olds in his office, he isn't as with it as he likes to think he is. They're facing no deadlines, none of his scheduled panic attacks. He can live without her. She needs a week. A novel a day, and a day of rest to ponder, a day to decide, and act. It's a very Wilkersonian plan, except his heroine would journey to five cities all over the globe, while Genevieve never leaves her studio apartment.

It's like she's fifteen again, just her and Sandy in her room curled up in one of his books, together.

Chapter Two

Theft

Genevieve Slidell, Author

Reader, I married him.

—Charlotte Bronte, Jane Eyre

They aren't at all what she expected, her five discoveries. As she eats the last muffin—an oily little concoction called an Everything Muffin that's grown a little rancid in a week—she ponders what to do with the novels. She's been thinking about it all along, of course, but each new novel made her rethink what she'd thought before, and now that she's read all five, she's not sure what to think. The sun is sinking low. Tomorrow's Monday. Back to work. She can't face Bent without a plan.

Not that she's about to hand these over to Bent. She's more sure about that than ever. He would so totally not get them. He would almost certainly hate them.

One theory about why Wilkerson quit writing novels is that he'd grown tired of the good old-fashioned novel for which he was known, that he longed to try something new—new themes, new genres—but his publishers weren't receptive, more like openly hostile. You don't mess with an established brand.

These five manuscripts lend credence to the longing theory, previously supported by a handful of pissy emails to his agent and editor, but he did more than long apparently, he wrote. They're all over the map, not a one of them a Wilkerson novel as she's come to think of it—different genres, different characters and plots, a willful disregard for setting (when the typical pan of a Wilkerson novel sneeringly uses the word *travelogue* at least once) but she has no doubt he wrote them. They still take her places she's never been—which is what he's always done. Geographically is the least of it. His sensibility oozes from every page, his view of the world, but older now, wiser perhaps, at times seemingly indulging a second childhood. Or maybe he just went crazy. He could still do it though—tell a story you can't put down, charm her into believing damn near anything. He blew her mind at fourteen when she stepped into his characters and had eight new lives to live, when before she'd been nobody, reading *The Awakening* and imagining wading into the Gulf. Now, thirteen years later, he's done it again. She thought she preferred her art straight ahead and down the middle until she read these.

She would have quite the critical task persuading the Wilkerson scholarly world—a tweedy stodgefest of tightasses who all hit on her at conferences (as if), but show absolutely no respect for her opinions—that these are Wilkerson's work, but she thinks she could pull it off. If she wanted.

But she doesn't. Want to. Feels it in her bones she shouldn't somehow. It doesn't seem right. He never revealed them to *anyone*. He clearly didn't want to. Novels don't appear out of thin air, they leave a huge paper trail. The notebooks, drafts, and miscellany generated by the first eight dwarfed the stack of books themselves. And Genevieve's read every swinging word, and there's not a peep about these five.

Nor is there a trace on his surviving hard drives. He never showed these manuscripts to his agent or editor or mentioned them in his chatty and often revealing emails with friends and lovers and fans. (He rarely wrote to relatives). Genevieve has read it all, annotated and indexed it all. She would know. He went on and on about the crappiest little sonnet he'd been working on to his pal Steve in Ypsilanti, but not a whisper of these. He kept them secret, said nothing. Why didn't you tell me? she wants to know. I would've understood. I may have been the only one who would!

And now *she's* the one who's found them. What are the odds? It was like a sacred moment or something. Soul mates reaching across time. She knows that last part is totally crazy, but Wilkersonian as hell, so she figures he wouldn't mind. He was a force in her soul mate search. No other guy could ever measure up. She's always thought it strange that his work is so middle-of-the-road, while his characters and his personal life were so quixotic and daring. Now she sees he had an outlet, a secret writing life, her five discoveries:

***

Missing Persons is a noir mystery involving a woman and a detective in search of her missing twin, a woman with whom the detective has long been in love, an obsession that destroyed his marriage. Though supposedly there's no love lost between him and the seeking twin, they have plenty of hot sex in various motels along the way searching for the missing one, saying things like

"You're not her."

"That's why you want me."

"Oh yeah? Why is it you want me?"

"Maybe I don't. Maybe I just want you to want me."

"Because of her."

"Everything is because of her."

Noir's not usually her genre, except for Chandler, who Sandy admired (and she devoured), but Genevieve is fascinated by the twins, by the detective enthralled by them. They all seem to be reaching for something real, and Genevieve can feel it inside herself—that reaching. The mystery doesn't matter to her. Maybe it never does. Good thing too. The ending is totally enigmatic—not a word that shows up often in Wilkerson criticism.

But there he is again, awakening feelings inside herself she didn't know were there. When she was a girl, she kept a notebook where she wrote them down—addressed to Sandy. She doesn't use the notebook anymore, though she still has it. She talks things over with him in her head. So, what's with the motel rooms? she plans to ask him first chance. Which twin am I, old friend? Which twin am I?

***

Scapegoat Phoenix is the story of Isaac after he escapes Abraham's mad attempt to murder him on God's orders. Set in a bizarre magical realist mash-up of the modern world and biblical times, the novel portrays Isaac as a desperate young man fleeing a contract on his life. In the opening sequence, he flags down a passing camel train weaving through stands of saguaro on its way into Phoenix, the lights from the Interstate glowing on the horizon. Fallen Angels are the new illegals, so all the roofers, road crews, maids, and nannies are winged, and everyone pretends not to notice so they won't be sent to Hell. Knowing he can't flee the will of God, Isaac decides to take a stand in Phoenix and starts organizing the fallen. The sun stands still over Phoenix. The temperature starts to rise. Everyone God has it in for from Job to Jezebel start showing up in town to take a stand.

In the published novels, there's a vague pantheist Zen thing going on that, like the scenic splendor, draws its share of scorn. Genevieve followed in his footsteps with her head down, navigating the Baptist hallways of her Texas high school. He alludes to the Bible on occasion, usually not in a flattering light, but she had no idea he was quite so pissed off at God. She remembers he went off about the plight of illegal immigrants once or twice in the emails, but nothing like this. She found her own rage on both fronts growing as she read. Turns out all those travelogue skills work even when the place is totally unreal. She's dying to go to Arizona and see the fallen angels and the saguaros. Both seemed equally real.

***

The Mad Statue, perhaps the strangest of all but also her fave, concerns a mad statue, Mirth, who magically becomes conscious and sets out to awaken her fellow statuary, also turning humans into statues occasionally, like *Cop Eating Donuts*, if she thought they might be happier. Some statues join her cause, others go their own way. Like Dorothy in *Oz*, she assembles quite a crew. Richmond has more than its share of statues. In an early scene, the Mad Statue makes her way down Monument Avenue setting the Confederate icons free, though she has to shrink the Godzilla sized Lee down to life size so as not to panic the populace. Lee and company seem unaware the Lost Cause is lost, the war over, since their makers didn't seem to know it, and mayhem ensues, but Mirth (the Mad Statue) makes things right. It's like a children's story with fangs. Genevieve imagines Monument Avenue, nothing but pedestals and dogs to piss on them left to remind. It'll be hard to face the far dopier heroic reality again. Wilkerson wrote this long before the current turmoil. It's amazing how timely it is, though it might have to be revised for a modern audience.

Willingly is a borderline pornographic sizzling romance that took her a little longer to get through than the others, with frequent recreational interruptions that further fueled her soul mate fantasies. There's so much sex on trains that, when she thinks about sex now, it sounds like the clatter of train wheels cutting through the night, wailing like a locomotive when she comes. The plot is some distraction about a controversial work of art, a painting. The heroine fucks almost everyone who might possibly have anything to do with it until the work of art turns out to be a forgery, the work of the artist she is posing for and most passionately fucking at novel's end. He has some disillusioned ideal behind his forging and is therefore forgiven for his deception. That's where the novel ends, in that happily-ever-after afterglow the genre requires, before the heroine has to climb out the bathroom window or stroll through galleries of her portrait as a shrew. Genevieve can understand the appeal. In light of her recent activities, she finds comfort in the fact that Sandy seemingly sides with the forger.

There's one intriguing detail. The painting is called *Lydia's Dream*, attributed in the novel to an invented famous impressionist, and depicts a boating party, a man at the oars and five women, all looking off, but not at each other. The heroine/artist's model bears a remarkable resemblance to the invented impressionist's favorite model, the focal point of the composition, who is inexplicably nude.

Lydia's Sandy's last wife's name. The descriptions of the painting make it clear it's him and his wives. If Lydia ever had such a dream, Genevieve doesn't know of it, but she does have to allow there must be many things she doesn't know about Sandy. Five wives is a lot of pillow talk.

It's the only one of the five manuscripts with a pseudonym: Chara Noon. That makes her smile. Chara was a beloved dog of his, a standard poodle who died at sixteen in his arms. Sandy gets choked up when he tells the story in a Morning Edition interview Genevieve's listened to dozens of times, getting weepy along with him. There are lots of shots of Sandy and Chara on the beach, in the woods, dancing at a party—both in party hats. Genevieve always wished she could've met her. She's happy Chara gets to lend her name to a romance. Sandy probably thought he needed a female name for the genre, even though the overwhelming majority of Sandy's readers were always women.

***

A Sandstorm of Destinies is a science fiction novel—a genre Wilkerson was fond of sneering at—about multiple realities twisting and turning like a hot yoga class with some of the characters from the other five showing up just to fuck with her head. The hero/heroine (this changes from one reality to the next) has come unstuck from her/his reality and cuts a swath across other worlds wreaking chaos. There's not so much sex as in some of the others because Dee, the heroine/hero keeps running afoul of the conflicting mores of each new world before anything can develop, as well as adjust to her kaleidoscopic gender identity. In the end, she's hopelessly confused, been everywhere but belongs nowhere. He steps out his door, and she's somewhere new.

Genevieve can relate:

She just opened a box and looked inside, and everything's changed. Though nothing's *really* changed but that these pages were moved, were read. Only her mind. Even if she put them back exactly as she found them except for the dust, everything would still have changed. Everything she thought she had figured out about the Wilkerson Novel before is off and doesn't matter anymore in ways she hasn't even thought of yet. But that's okay. Better somehow. A clean slate. A new Genevieve. Better to be wrong or plain clueless than stupid and not know it.

Her dissertation in progress (?) is about Wilkerson's vagabonds.

There are still vagabonds everywhere you look in the discovered five, but they're a different breed from those in the published eight.

Where they need to go isn't Tahiti or Siberia or the canals of Venice—someplace in the latest editions of *Lonely Planet*. It's more likely a park in the moonlight, a semi into Phoenix, or someplace, anyplace, just so we get there *soon*, to fuck and question the nature of reality.

No one flies, not counting the Mad Statue who gets around by having herself shipped Fed-Ex, and some of that's in jets, but there's not a single airport scene. The published eight pass through dozens of airports: She has a whole chapter on airports. The characters here mostly ride in trains, and of course, they go for long walks in the woods. In *Sandstorm* one of the characters laments he's been to dozens of realities, and not a one has hovercars, but they all have trains. The lucky ones have woods outside the windows.

Missing Persons is a road trip that shuns the Interstates, following the routes the twins' father took as a traveling salesman when their mother and the twins went along in the summers. The missing twin is mysteriously obsessed with reliving those trips from their youth. The detective and the seeking twin are always a few days behind. The car is old, the motels and diners old, the owners new. The owners come from everyplace unfortunate enough to be in the news. *Refugees buy motels*, the detective observes, *so they'll always have a place to sleep*. The motel owners remember the missing twin, but having been refugees, they hesitate to help the pursuers of someone in flight. *Look at her. You doubt she is her sister?* the detective asks, pointing to the seeking twin. A Syrian in Arkansas replies, *Perhaps she is the same woman who once told me she has no family, and she is the one you seek. Perhaps I am not the man my brother in Damascus would deny exists.*

Orphaned ambiguities. Like these novels. They never had a chance back when they were written. Even if he'd published them, they would've been the target of critical scorn as too offbeat for the best-selling author. The BSA as Sandy called it when he felt particularly hemmed in by fame. And what would happen now if they surfaced after all these years?

She imagines the MLA sessions *ad nauseam*. They would be a curiosity, a sideshow, a symptom of his declining powers in old age—too much was invested in good old reliable GSW to take them seriously. Bent would hate them. A dead writer should have the decency to stay dead and not contradict everything that was ever concluded about him. Add to the mix the assholes who never thought Wilkerson deserved the rise in his reputation since his death who would savage these new works on principle, the science fiction people who would have their revenge on *Sandstorm* with a shit storm of their own, and the religious right who would go totally berserk over *Scapegoat*—the novels themselves wouldn't stand a chance with his name on them. Sandy may have known what he was doing when he shoved them into the darkest corner of his attic to be forgotten.

Maybe—just a thought—she could say *she* wrote them.

They lie before her, five stacks on a card table, her desk she calls it, not one to invest in furniture since she's always on the cusp of moving on. She touches the title pages, imagines Genevieve Slidell there instead. Sandy wouldn't mind. He'd probably prefer it, that an adventure be made of them by a plucky heroine giving them a chance to live instead of abandoning them to Bent and his crew to turn into lifeless artifacts of academe, battlefields for intellectual armies warring for tenure and promotion.

If, however, they were the work of a brilliant young woman—who, though she bombed spectacularly in the only creative writing class she ever took, swearing she'd never take another, *wanted* to write brilliantly just as badly as any of her seemingly more talented boyfriends ever had—they might stand a chance. She loved literature so much it was obviously the most incredible hubris to imagine she could create it. In her experience, the more talented the writer, the bigger fuckoff he or she is. Genevieve isn't lazy; she just has zero talent. She can't remember the details, and doesn't care to recall them, but her manuscripts dripped brutal red ink, and she remembers what it added up to: Zero. "I don't usually say this," her instructor told her, "but you have absolutely no talent for fiction." He was being kind, he claimed, to spare her lifelong frustration. Gee thanks.

She can't help herself though. She keeps writing anyway. Occasionally she retests herself by sharing some smidgin of her work, something she's not too invested in, with a new writer boyfriend who, to their credit, each and every one, confirms she has no talent. Too tentative, too strident, too this, too that. It varied with the boyfriend. Not so much to her credit, she's dumped them soon after. Just a *smidge* of validation with the sex—is that too much to ask? To be fair, she did beg them to be honest. She did not say, however, brutally honest.

Wilkerson, it's now clear to Genevieve, possessed more talent than a single lifetime could contain. The most treasured experience of her life has been reading Wilkerson's work. She owes him for all the hours she's spent in his fictional worlds to give these new guys a shot. She'll shepherd these orphaned works into the world so that they get the recognition they deserve. Wilkerson once said, "Novelists are mostly shits. It's only the novels that matter."

Exactly.

Genevieve looks forward to rereading them again and again, her five novels, plunging into their depths. She would like nothing better than to luxuriate in these new worlds, ride in trains and fuck in motels, in hot pursuit of meaningful mysteries, flipping off God in the desert, gender surfing though alt universes (written before anyone said alt). Love and justice and joy—but most of all adventure, another wild ride with the perfect stranger.

But first things first. First, she needs to make them hers, adopt them as her own.

Okay, she admits to the rearview mirror when she gets into the car with the box of novels riding shotgun—steal them.

***

She drives down to the university, near deserted on a Sunday night, with the manuscripts and her last pizza to nuke, holes up in the *Wilkerson Studies* office, good little drone that she is, pulling another all-nighter. She makes a pot of coffee. Campus Security stops by, and she gives him a slice and a cup. His name's Dave. He's hot for her, or maybe he's hot for any woman he finds working alone at 2 a.m. Genevieve gets lonely from the inside out.

While they discuss the rash of robberies in the neighborhood lately, she tends to the document feeder, scanning the manuscripts and turning them into Word files on her laptop that could've been written yesterday. By her. She backs them up in the Cloud where they've never been before. When Dave's gone, she researches strategies for breaking into print and decides contests may be the way to go. Agents and editors might have too many probing questions and spot her for the phony she is. In a contest, it's just the book, on its own. Pure fiction.

This idea has a certain appeal since Sandy launched his career by winning a contest at thirty with *Death By Beauty*, which he wrote between his second and third marriage while laid up in Belize with a broken leg from an accident sustained while crewing for some drunken yachtsman. *Death* is rough, but in some ways his most intense work. The reviewers liked the story of its composition as much as they liked the novel itself, and the camera and microphone both adored him. He took his new vocation seriously, saying he was surprised to discover that he possessed a gift, but he did not intend to squander it.

That's her man. And she doesn't intend to squander it either. Do you think if an incredibly zany musical comedy written by Melville or Kafka were unearthed that it would ever see the lights of Broadway? Not likely. Who would show up on *Today* to pitch it? Ishmael? Gregor? These orphaned novels need someone young and interesting to smile into the camera and say, *I made these.*

By dawn, she's mapped out a plan, a list of the most prestigious contests suitable to her rich and varied oeuvre. Some want the whole thing. Some want the first few chapters. Some require a physical manuscript. Most want electronic submissions. Some want bios. Most don't care if you come from Pluto. There are forms and cover letters and format specifications. But with the resources and facilities of the *Wilkerson Studies* office at her disposal, she's able to complete the task in no time, tossing the last manuscript into outgoing snail mail as the hallways start coming to life as classes begin. She looks around her domain, the shelves of past issues, the portrait of Sandy on the wall shot by Lydia's sister-in-law. He's 46, handsome as he ever was. He had fourteen years to live.

She imagines the last ten, up in that cabin, showing the world what he could do beside the sexy vagabonds, then hiding it away, wiping out every trace of them. Did he save the copies she found that had somehow survived the general purge, or did he simply forget them?

They don't deserve to be forgotten. She has faith in them. One of them *has* to win something, and she'll be there to tell the world, there's more where that came from.

It's not as if she doesn't have some skin in the game. She hates the expression—an old boyfriend often used it, and she winced every time—but likes the idea. Most of these things have entry fees that add up to the last nails in the coffin of her last surviving credit card. She should just cut it up right now and be done with it. A small price to pay for the powerful surge of hope that the story of her life might not turn out to be dull and pointless after all, that in this weird and wonderful way she's found a means to do something for the love of her life, who never even knew she was alive.

She knows—she's not an idiot—that this is probably right up there with spending every dime on the lottery because you dreamed the winning numbers, but the way she has it figured, the story goes like this: Genius is genius. At least one of the five will win. She has faith in him, and in their five children launched into the world after a long and mysterious slumber. It's positively mythic, like Moses in the bulrushes. Now she has to wait, the hardest part. Sandy hated this part, waiting for judgment. He often complained of it in his correspondence. She just has to put it out of her mind. "Good luck with that," she says to Sandy on the wall.

She has one more immediate task to perform, and she cannot hesitate, because she knows if she does, she won't do it. Now that she's claimed them all for her own—under a variety of pseudonyms consisting of favorite but obscure Wilkerson characters—the original copies from Wilkerson could possibly land her in jail if they were ever discovered. He kept them secret, and she must also. She shreds them. The machine emits a sound like a long, sustained scream as it chews through the five, one right after another—over 1500 pages—until they're gone. She breaks down the box and puts it in the recycling bin, including the lid she's tempted to keep with Wilkerson's own scrawled acronyms for the novels he stuck in the attic like Rochester's wife, but resists. She's done it now. No turning back. No souvenirs. No tags back, as they used to say when she was a kid. Kid no more, she thinks. Oh my God, what have I done?

Chapter Three

Confession

Don't Look Back

"Villains!' I shrieked. 'Dissemble no more! I admit the deed! Tear up the planks! Here, here! It is the beating of his hideous heart!"
— *Edgar Allan Poe, "The Tell-Tale Heart"*

The latest crop of writers are all too young for her, so she's been nursing along a relationship with a Coleridge scholar named Clint they both know isn't going anywhere. He just started a three-year instructorship; she's determined to finish her dissertation this year. This simply isn't a good time. Neither's motivated to move on or give it up, so they simply drift.

He's something of a relief after the Creative Nonfiction guy working on his memoir at thirty-five who practiced telling all with Genevieve while she wished he wouldn't, but didn't want to staunch the flow. He told her she had become an indispensable part of his process. What girl doesn't dream of that? Clint doesn't talk about his past much at all. Mostly he talks about Samuel Taylor Coleridge and his friends. When he's feeling frisky, he talks about Keats.

It's Tuesday night, discount night at the movies. Tomorrow, it's a week and a half since she did it——stole those manuscripts from a dead man and said they were hers, and not just any dead man, but the closest thing to a saint in her agnostic (okay, atheist) life. As you can see, she's had *way* too much time to think about it and nothing but it, so help her God, ever since.

She's awash in guilt. She started a letter to all the contests, confessing her deceit, detailing her subterfuge, but insisting on the authenticity of the manuscripts as the long-lost work of a great novelist, when she realized what would happen next. They'd be yanked from all the competitions, probably discredited as being anything Wilkerson would've ever written, just the half-baked product of some crazy from Texas. End of story. All five of them.

She has to let them win, keep them in the game. She doesn't see how she can just yank them now. If they win, they have to be taken seriously, no matter who wrote them. That's the time to come clean.

She and Clint have seen a movie neither liked. Her choice, since he wouldn't decide. She chose it because there were no superheroes or serial killers, and she usually likes the actor despite his macho swagger. Not tonight. He spent most of the movie on a bicycle. She spent the whole thing wanting him to be crushed under a bus or a street cleaner.

Now they're trying the new Thai. Genevieve's Thaied out, and they're tired of trashing the movie. Clint's nervous, sensing she's not all there, and is telling her the story he's apparently forgotten he told her on their first date of how he came to be a Coleridge scholar in the first place, when a young charismatic high school English teacher named Harry Dawson did a whiz bang job with *The Rime of the Ancient Mariner* and wowed the young Clint. Thirty-somethings telling stories from their youth annoy Genevieve. You should be at least fifty to reminisce on a date.

It's not his fault. All she can think about are her five kidnapped children out in the world, waiting to be read and judged, like the Mariner becalmed on that damn boat. She wants them to win—how can she not want that? But then what? She goes back and forth. The guilt could be overwhelming if she persists in the lie that she wrote them, or this could be a dream come true. The contests are all announced within a few weeks of one another, their respective ceremonies, hosted by some convention or other, come one right after another. Genevieve wonders whether there's some genre event coordinator who makes sure they don't overlap. But who writes in five genres? Sandy. Now she's even more impressed with him than before—which she didn't think possible. Will she know how to pretend to be a Real Writer if she has to? She thinks so. She's known a lot of young writers. She just has to remember not to be too happy, not to know too much about what it all means. Writers don't seem to care about that as much as she would've thought. Want to piss off a poet? Ask him what one of his lines means. Especially in bed. Might as well deconstruct his cock while you're at it.

She interrupts Clint's ongoing inspirational tale near the big finish when he borrows the Doré illustrated edition and poured over it pretty much forever with occasional breaks to become Professor Clinton Cross. "Did you ever just want to *be* Samuel Taylor Coleridge?"

He tilts his head to one side, smiles dreamily. The idea captures his imagination immediately. Clint's easy that way, one of his better qualities. If you want to take a flight of fancy—Genevieve's favorite kind—Clint's usually onboard. "I could take long walks through the Lake District with William and Dorothy."

She rolls her eyes. Why is everyone so hot for Dorothy? "I don't mean like that. You wouldn't really want to *live* back then. No electricity. No modern medicine. Open sewers. Most of your so-called expertise would be useless. You'd hate it and die young. I mean, to *be* somebody who could *write* something like that. Just you and the words. He wrote a poem you've practically based your whole life on. Forget suspension of disbelief. How incredible is *that?*" She realizes she's holding a chopstick like it's a conductor's baton and she's about to cue the crashing cymbals. She puts it down, folds her hands, one over the other.

He's never looked at her before quite the way he does in the wake of this passionate outburst, and she realizes she's never revealed much of herself to Clint before but flesh and wit, mostly dry. No heart, not one little bit. It feels good, so she says apropos of his bedazzled gaze, "So you want to go to your place?" She tears open her fortune cookie.

He tries to hide his surprise. Things didn't seem to be going in that direction only moments ago. What could he have done right? He's immediately crestfallen, however. He hangs his head and shakes it. "I can't."

"Can't?"

"My mother's visiting, passing through on business. It was last minute. I told her I already had plans. She's sleeping in my bed. I'm on the couch." He cracks open his fortune, reads, scowls and gobbles the cookie down. He closes his fist around his fortune. She imagines it a soggy little wad inside.

"What does it say?"

"*Love comes to he who waits.*" How to describe his smile? Doesn't matter. She's not describing; she's feeling. Touched.

He's never spent the night at her place. The official line is it's too small. They both know she prefers the control of leaving when she wants. She blames the *brujo* for that. Clint must've guessed she has privacy issues as well. The restaurant's close to the deck where her car is parked—why she chose it. He's assuming she'll have him walk her to her car and say good night. His disappointment is monumental. So near, and yet so far. Poor guy. "Is Mom expecting you? Maybe you should give her a call." She gives Clint an unmistakable smile.

Clint beams and picks up his phone without a moment's hesitation. She likes a man who isn't afraid to level with his mom.

Trying not to listen to just how he tells Mom he's hooking up to-night, Genevieve reads her fortune: *When crossroads flood, another way must be found.* She starts to wad hers, too, but decides to keep it to ponder later. She can't decide if it's just the traffic report or something profound. Cue the symbols.

Clint, his hand on her knee, says, "Let's go."

***

When he's following her home, his headlights in her rearview, Gen-evieve realizes where this is going, why she's taking Clint home. It feels like a big dead albatross just slipped from her neck and disappeared in her wake. She can't carry this guilt around alone. She has to stop a wedding guest and share. Clint will understand. It's his favorite story.

Wilkerson's wandering characters are often far away from home and form quick, intense liaisons with near strangers. They're usually wan-dering with a secret or two festering in their hearts aching for release, in addition to their raging libidos. Often, before or after some of the afore-mentioned sex, they tell all, like a confession, the reverberations from which fuel the remaining plot of the novel and the moral development of the character. She's applied this stratagem in her own life with mixed results. It has been eventful, but perhaps she's not the one to address the moral development of her character. Confession's good, right? Then maybe he'll talk some sense into her. Or at least try.

Maybe it's the inspiration of having been invited into her hermit's cave or the knowledge that Mom knows he's getting laid, but Clint out-does himself by a good measure, and she's in no mood to hold anything back after a spectacular orgasm.

She tells him *everything*.

She even tells him about the shredder. She will never, ever, as long as she lives, forget the shredder. She imitates its shriek.

She *even* tells him about her dreams of being a writer. She feels worst about that, trying to justify what she's done. Who cares about her fucking dreams? Everyone has dreams. She already knows the worst of it is that even if she gets to pretend she's a writer, she won't really be one. She figures he'll point this out to her. She has a whole list of things in her head he might point out. Despite his predilection for romantic poetry, he's a pretty down-to-earth guy.

Of all the things she thinks he'll say, what he does say isn't one of them. "Can I read them?" He looks ghoulishly fascinated, as if they were corpses buried in the basement.

"I don't know. I guess. It doesn't bother you?"

He's admiring her naked body, smiling. Why is he smiling? "That your ghost writer is really a ghost?"

"C'mon. No joke. What I did. It was awful. Unforgivable. I don't know what came over me. It was *wrong*." She wants him to stop her any time. He does.

He touches her lips with his fingertips. "I suppose so, but it doesn't matter—because I love you, Genevieve. So very much." He looks into her eyes when he says this. The fingertips flee her stunned lips—so she can speak. Nothing rushes out.

Okay. This is even more unexpected. "Don't say that. We just had great sex. That's all." She caresses his face with her hands, sending something of a mixed message, but it *was* really great sex, and she teared up when he said what he said, but not in a bad way. *Loves* her? How did she miss it? Don't answer that.

"And you confessed a felony to me," he says, touching the space between her breasts as if maybe her soul does live there. The heart chakra or whatever it is her yoga teacher's always on about. It's beaming into deep space: *Om-m-m*.

"You think?" she whispers.

"Definitely. More than one, I'd say. Claiming authorship, then destroying them. Five counts of each."

"Mmm. All the more reason you can't, you know . . . What you said." Her voice trembles a little. She stops herself. Totally uncalled for.

He smiles sweetly, still bedazzled. He does pretty well with rejection apparently, or he's not listening. "If you would confess something like that, trust me that much, you must have feelings for me," he says. "I see no reason to conceal my own. I think about you all the time. I can't bear the thought of being without you. I would follow you anywhere."

No man has ever said anything remotely resembling this to Genevieve before, not unless you count its inverse—don't *ever* come anywhere near me again, you crazy bitch. Clint had trouble deciding between soup or drunken noodles, he didn't care what movie they saw, but he seems certain of *this*? Genevieve speaks reason, though it's not her first language: "You're into the romantics, Clint. You're terribly sweet, but you don't think rationally. I'm flattered, but I have to confess I can't keep a secret. It could've been *anybody*. Really." This isn't true, and she knows it, but she tries to sell it. She doesn't see herself with a Coleridge scholar. Big brown eyes. Hands caressing her thighs, a whole other chakra.

"Right," he says, and they make love some more.

Genevieve can now more fully understand the appeal of the heartfelt confession. She's never had so much to confess before. Her felonies have inspired him. His inspiration inspires her. She's forced to admit he's not just anybody. She could get used to this, but has the feeling she shouldn't. It's always forever with some guys, doesn't mean they'll stick around. Always love—even when it's not.

She's always seen herself with some version of Sandy or other, but now that she's pretended to be five versions of him herself, she sees no reason she can't think outside the box. Maybe she needs someone to help keep her grounded. Like a guy who's pursued his high school obsession with a screwy poem about a mystical vagabond who once shot an albatross and never got over it, right on into being a rootless scholar gypsy with a Ph.D. Her ghost writer would approve.

Clint gets promoted in her mind to boyfriend. Part of the new Genevieve, the new well-fucked Genevieve. She takes a long, hot shower. When she emerges, he sets down the phone.

"Just checking on Mom," he says.

Such a good lad, loves his mum, surely not a bad sign. She crawls into bed beside him and soon falls fast asleep. She hasn't slept so well since she found the five manuscripts and changed her life, stole them and changed it again. She has a flying dream, usually one of her favorites. She's a soaring albatross. She can't help constantly anticipating a shaft piercing her heart, plunging into the wide salt sea.

***

In the morning, he asks her after more sex, "Would you like to meet my mother?" and she remembers the downside of the boyfriend thing. "I'm meeting her for breakfast at Joe's Inn. She flies out this afternoon."

The new Genevieve is lying on top of him, a puddle of bliss, when he asks her this, and she says she'd be delighted, hopes she'll be anyway. Clint claims Genevieve will like his mother and vice versa, not a claim in Genevieve's experience, every son will make. Those who have haven't proven entirely correct. Perhaps Clint will claim another first.

What a night.

"What's Mom do?" she asks him. She's been toweling off, getting dressed, and he's been looking at her like she's Venus in the shallows. If he keeps looking at her like that, they may have to give Mom another call.

"She's a detective."

"Jeez. What kind?"

"DEA."

"No shit?"

He laughs hard. "I'm just kidding. She's a detective, but she's private. Tracks down runaways mostly. Started with my big sister Chloe who took off when I was thirteen. She was fifteen. Never found her, but my mom had all these skills she acquired looking. She took courses, got a license. She's pretty good at it. Semi-famous."

"Is that what she's doing here? Tracking someone down?"

"Yeah. She had to talk to someone's granny who turned out not to know anything."

"I bet granny just didn't want to squeal on her Little Pumpkin."

Clint shrugs, still looking at her like he can't believe his good fortune that she should care for him, in spite of her multiple felonies and deplorable character. "I don't know. Little Pumpkin stole her car once and totaled it. My Mom's got a pretty good bull shit detector. You look great by the way."

"No way, but thanks. I'm sorry about your sister."

"Pissed me off. We were pretty close. You remind me of her."

"Great."

He laughs. "Like that."

She knows he doesn't remember his father, that he left when Clint was two. Mad at Dad was an early bond. This is the first she's heard of sister Chloe. Genevieve guesses they're not going to have any secrets now. Fewer anyway. She's met her confession quota for now. Five felonies vs. one missing sister: Shouldn't he be telling her more?

***

Breakfast goes well, better than well. Tanya, Clint's mother, looks more like a librarian than a detective, a little plump, smiley and chatty. Inquisitive, Genevieve notices. Definitely curious. Whether this is the detective thing or the Mom thing, Genevieve's uncertain. Maybe Tanya suspects this isn't like Genevieve to even be here. Genevieve can't help noticing Tanya's subtle, accepting smile is not unlike her son's. She wants to trust them, but isn't quite sure she should.

Tanya asks her about future plans, as mothers will, and after the usual mumblings about her dissertation, Genevieve explains she's also a novelist with several irons in the fire. Genevieve blames this extravagant claim on the mimosas Tanya insisted she join her in drinking. Clint, as the driver, abstains. Tanya's scarcely touched hers, while nervous Genevieve's has vanished. Sober Clint, when asked if he's read Genevieve's work, lies without hesitation that he has read some and found it quite wonderful and is looking forward to reading the new stuff. Genevieve likes a man who'll lie to his mother for love, especially so convincingly. When Tanya goes to the bathroom, Genevieve thanks him for the falsehood.

"I didn't lie. You can't lie to her. I've read a couple of Wilkerson's novels. They were wonderful, and I do hope to read these new ones." He corrects himself: "Yours."

"Which Wilkerson's did you read?"

"I read *Don't* in high school. I had a crush on a girl who told me it was the best book in the whole world. I read *The Forest of Forgetfulness* when I first got here."

"How come?"

"You were carrying around a copy at the departmental meeting."

"So basically you read modern fiction to get girls, but otherwise prefer 19th-century poetry?"

He laughs. "Something like that."

"Do you plan to tell your mom your girlfriend's a liar and a thief?"

"Are you my girlfriend?" This pleases him no end.

Mom finds them kissing in the booth on her return, and she smiles approvingly. Soon after, Clint's ex, Barbara, comes up in the conversation. Tanya carves her up like her sausages. Clint pours syrup on his pancakes and tries to change the subject, but there's no stopping her message to Genevieve: I like you way better than the last one, but don't ever get on my bad side.

When they're about to leave, waiting for the waitress to return with Tanya's credit card, Clint slips off to the Men's, and Tanya smiles at Genevieve. "What are you running from, dear?"

Suddenly the loud, clattering restaurant gets very small and quiet, like the dark corner of an abandoned attic. For a brief, endless moment Genevieve thinks somehow Tanya knows what she's done, but that's impossible. She starts to say she's not running from anything, but the question has so clearly rattled her, there's no denying it now. She decides to go with the truth, some of it at least: "I've done something awful I can't undo that may benefit me greatly. I didn't hurt anybody or anything, but it was still awful. I can't believe I did it, but I can't deny I want those benefits. I don't know what to think of myself since I did it. I guess that's what I'm running from. Me."

Tanya doesn't ask her what awful thing she's done, doesn't even seem interested in that part of the equation, only the lost soul. "You poor thing. Well, I'm sure you'll figure it out. You seem quite capable. You can count on Clint." She lays her hands on Genevieve's. "He's true." She looks up and smiles wide. "And here he is. You promised me Monument Avenue before I go. I hope you don't mind, dear?" She adds this last to Genevieve, including her in Genevieve's least favorite Richmond visitor ritual.

"Great," Genevieve manages, rising beside Clint and clinging to his arm, already dreading facing the icons back on their pedestals. The Mad Statue had the right idea. Set the bastards free. It's hard to keep a Lost Cause down. Like acid reflux, it will rise again.

Throughout the journey from Stuart to Stonewall and beyond, Tanya acts like they have a secret between the two of them, she and Genevieve: *Clint's true.* Genevieve watches him being the good son, orbiting General Lee like Captain Kirk showing a Vulcan diplomat a barbaric planet and wonders if it's true. So, what's he doing with Genevieve the Novel Thief? How can a true one be with someone who's not? Now that he knows.

He lets her off at her place, kisses and hugs all around, then mother and son head for the airport. She wants to curl up and read her novels, see if she can find herself there like she did when she read them the first time, making it easier to steal them somehow, because she was *there*, in the pages. He was speaking to *her*.

But she can't bring herself to face them quite yet. What if they say to her, *you don't belong here*?

She works instead on her dissertation, penance of sorts. Lit crit is like Scrabble to her. She's pretty good at it, but she doesn't really like it that much. She loves to play Monopoly but can never get enough people to play and almost never wins. Now that she knows the five novels that come after she reached all her conclusions about Wilkerson, everything she's concluded about him seems like total bullshit. She starts striking things out at a pretty scary clip and stops herself before she deletes the whole thing.

Needing some real torture, she turns to the editing of the articles for the next issue of *Wilkerson Studies*—smug, erudite, and wrong, wrong, wrong.

At bedtime she rereads some Du Maurier, a Sandy favorite. *Don't Look Back* seems appropriate.

***

And so it goes.

It's a long, cold winter.

Except for Clint, sweet Clint.

He's true.

And her children. She soon makes her peace with them. Reads and rereads them until she's reading nothing else like some people read a sacred book. Events in her day remind her of certain scenes; people in her life, she associates with particular characters; she forgets sometimes that none of them are real. She imagines discussing all this with interviewers—the teeming regions of her vast imagination. She forgets sometimes she stole them. They seem to have seeped inside of her. She can't give them back. At this point, they won't let her go.

She's become obsessed with statues. Once you start looking, they're everywhere. She imagines them coming to life, trying to figure out who they are. Sometimes she imagines people turning into statues with names like *Waiting, Lost,* and *Checked Out.* One morning she walked out of her place and everything was one big statue, *Things As They Are.* She stopped, astonished, taking it all in. She imagines lawn lions and porch labs in holiday gear coming to life and wonders what the first thing they'd do might be.

One of the interns for *Wilkerson Studies* lets it slip she's a twin while Genevieve is rereading *Missing Persons*, and Genevieve is so inquisitive about it, the girl complains to Bent, who knows better than to discipline Genevieve, but asks, "What is it with you and the twin thing?" He seems to think it's sexual, or maybe he was just being hopeful. He's been buzzing around the intern himself ever since.

Genevieve sees a sandstorm on TV rolling over Laredo and spends days researching sandstorms, realizing along the way Wilkerson must've done the same to come up with some of the imagery in *Sandstorm of Destinies*. She spends nights roaming the streets of Phoenix with the Google Man looking for camels and moneychangers, fallen angels at the bus stops.

Clint has read and loved them too, though he's not so sure about *The Mad Statue*. He might say that because he's in love with her and would rather not believe her favorite character is a mad, morphing hunk of marble on the loose with a penchant for inappropriate meanings and casual seductions. His favorite is *Scapegoat Phoenix*. He wants to go to Arizona first chance they get so they can check out the saguaros. The two of them take an overnight train to New Orleans during winter break, reenacting scenes from *Willingly* with absolute fidelity to the text. She's living in five magical worlds at once. Six, if you count the real one.

If she's going to steal them, shred them, then pray for their resurrection, the least she can do is go a little fanatical with them. Every waking moment she's plunging into them, like diving for pearls. She holds them up to the swine swaggering through Wilkerson scholarship like hogs in their wallow and says, *You don't understand him at all!* They even show up in her dreams. Characters. Whole scenes. Wilkerson often spoke of living whatever novel he was writing. It was like that, but five at once.

But so far nothing from Wilkerson himself. Not yet. Clint knows better than to make the ghost writer joke after the once, but part of her keeps waiting for Sandy to show up and say . . . what? *You thieving cunt!* or *You brilliant savior! Only you understand me now!* She supposes his reaction to being understood might go either way. She's not sure what he'd think of being entered in more than a dozen contests, whether he'd feel sullied or flattered. She strongly suspects the latter.

She's come to realize she understands him like no one else possibly can, for she alone has seen his secret self, become him in a sense, the embodiment of the work the world unwisely suppressed, giving it a new chance at life. She still feels awful about what she's done, but not a single day goes by without a famous author fantasy flitting through her brain like a Tourette's attack. She wants to win. She's *destined* to win. She knows this is magical thinking old Genevieve would scorn, but new Genevieve embraces this craziness as a sign of her faith, her cult of one. She's living the story of herself.

When several of the contests that had wanted only the opening chapters request the rest of the novels, this adds abundant fuel to the five fires. She tries not to think overly about burning in them.

Eventually she puts the dissertation away altogether, the pretense of working on it, and waits. She imagines her stunned and tearful response at the good news over and over again, like Mel Gibson reimagining the crucifixion. She's decided Sandy wants to win too. Vindication. Validation. Victory. She thinks a little too much like the Mad Statue sometimes. She's prayed to him. To Sandy. She hasn't forgotten him, knows he's dead and all of that, but she has to at least ask the man, *Is all this okay with you?*

She thinks she heard a laugh once, typical Sandy slyness. She took this to mean, *Sure, why not?* Or maybe it was, *What choice do I have?*

Chapter Four

Epiphany

He's Alive! He's Alive!

"It is true, we shall be monsters, cut off from all the world; but on that account we shall be more attached to one another."
— *Mary Wollstonecraft Shelley, Frankenstein*

Richmond is beautiful in the spring. Trees explode with blossoms up and down its avenues. The river is a glorious silver serpent in the sun. Genevieve feels as if the trees are blossoming for her, for Sandy. Their triumph is meant to be, as relentless as the rushing waters. She talks so much about Sandy, Clint complains he's getting jealous. She laughs, reminding him Sandy was dead before she knew who he even was. She doesn't tell him the soul mate business or the erotic fantasies. Boyfriends don't really want to hear about erotic fantasies. Destiny is bad enough.

Her grand notions are confirmed when the letters and phone calls start coming in. Two winners—*Scapegoat Phoenix* (Literary) and *A Sandstorm of Destinies* (Science Fiction)—and two runners-up—*Willingly* (Romance) and *Missing Persons* (Mystery). Most of the contests were for unknowns like her. Sandy couldn't even have entered but one or two if he were alive. He needed her to do this for him. She feels justified, validated—for the both of them—crazier than ever.

Nobody gets *The Mad Statue* apparently, except for Genevieve. It's still her favorite, but it rates no more than form letters. She imagines herself as a winged *Triumphant* anyway. She checks her calendar. Fortunately, none of the award ceremonies conflict. It's several months before the first one. Time to get ready, time to freak out. They pay her way, give her prize money. Nothing huge, but you can get prizewinners published, right? She crafts a resignation letter to Bent telling him to go fuck himself because she's going to be famous, or something to that effect. Keywords include *pathetic*, *creepy*, and *douche bag*. When you don't ever want to be tempted by a bridge again, you burn it or blow it up. That's just simple chemistry.

She hopes Clint knew what he was getting into when he said he'd follow her anywhere. He'll be delighted to see the last of the awards ceremonies is in Tucson. They have saguaros there, don't they?

***

She has one more self-indulgence to indulge, or perhaps it's a ritual of the highest spiritual significance. She feels compelled before she collects the honors for his orphaned novels as her own—to return to the scene of her crime, the mountain place, to stand where he stood one last time and try to get herself right with the universe, with Sandy. She has the keys; she made copies.

She imagines she's seeking her better twin out here, the Genevieve who didn't do it, who did what she was supposed to do and funneled Wilkerson's last five novels into the chute of academic understanding, like the last Twinkies coming off the line. As a result of her deceit, they've slipped that sacrificial altar, escaped the knife, fled the judgment of the gods. Instead, they're Winners, Runners-Up, her Personal Favorite—beats boxed up in the attic, doesn't it? To see the light of day, to greet adoring eyes?

Now the sun's shining on her, the author, the priestess, the thief of souls—wicked Jezebel. Jezebel shows up twice in the five novels—as her biblical counterpart stranded on a train broken down in Phoenix like a lot of other people God has it in for in *Scapegoat Phoenix*, and as a symbolic statue in *The Mad Statue*, renamed and reanimated by Mirth to be her staunchest ally. In both novels, she's the woman Genevieve wishes sometimes she had the guts to be, taking chances and never looking back, just going for it, which you may have the mistaken impression she is because of recent events, but compared to Jezebel, she's a sneaky little coward. So, feeling like Jezebel is a major step up.

It's an intoxicating persona. The twisting mountain road feels just dangerous enough, and she can't look back anyway unless she wants to go flying over the edge. She imagines herself getting new wheels with some of the prize money, something more like Sandy would drive, a convertible, or maybe a motorcycle, though she remembers him once complaining of the noise. Today it's probably a little too chilly for either one. Winter hangs on up here. Genevieve hates to be cold.

Sandy must've made this journey hundreds of times. A couple of the motels, now abandoned, made their way into *Missing Persons*, transplanted to a stretch of highway in east Texas on the edge of a town too small to have an edge. Much of *Willingly* seems to roll through this country, though he invented train lines where none exist, just so Deidre, the heroine, can fuck on another sleeper car. She remembers a particularly ebullient email after an overnight train ride to Boston with Lydia once that doesn't mention sex, but the inspiration seems obvious now. She used to pretend to be Lydia. He was happiest with her.

Everything, she imagines, went into the novels he made, from deep inside to the landscape gliding by. A million secrets she can never know. How will she explain herself, explain her adopted children, as she claims these prizes? Already, the knowledge that she's not worthy stings like lashes, making her feel momentarily like she's paying for it somehow, suffering for her art, but she knows that's bullshit of the highest order even as she's thinking it.

She's bullshit.

She imagines herself a statue: *Bullshit Kneeling.* A winged, artless, penitent turd.

She parks in the high grass and gets out. No one's been here. The University is still dithering about what they're going to do with it, which means it will sit here indefinitely. Just as well. She always imagined it smelled like him—woodstove and old pine boards, rat piss and genius and hours and hours alone.

That's what she's stolen—all those hours of solitude in the woods wrestling with his demons. The words were the least of it. She doesn't want to go inside. She's violated his memory enough. She's spent half her life with Sandy—his fan, his lover, his sixth wife. Crazy. But this, what is this? Pretending to be *him*? Blasphemy? Betrayal? Batshit Fucking Nuts?

She has to tell the truth. She has to confess they're his.

The fan on the Saturn finally cuts off, and it's near silent but for the babble of the creek by the house and the cry of a hawk up along the ridge. She wades through the high grass, mindful of snakes—there are copperheads and rattlers up here—and makes for the porch.

She kneels on the well-worn boards and confesses to the meadow, to the mountains, to the woods where she has long wandered, lingered, made love in the high grass—the world her beloved Sandy made real to her. The man she's betrayed. She hoped success would lessen that burden, that it would feel like his triumph too, but she only feels worse.

Most of all, she confesses to *him*, her first love, crush, whatever you want to call him, who has been dead the whole time. My God, he died right out there, keeled over in the noonday sun. Alone. This isn't the first time she's spoken to him, but never unloaded at such length. At least Clint had the good sense to hook his wagon to a nutty poem, not a nutty author. Genevieve's dentist father left a week after she started fifth grade to marry his pregnant hygienist, start a new family, and promptly forget her. You get the picture. Trust issues. Daddy issues. Issue issues. Sandy and only Sandy helped her wade through all those issues. She's over herself and her issues. There's no fucking forgiving what she's done.

She's so sorry. And scared. His novels have won these honors, and she's taken credit for them because she thought that would be best or she just wanted to leech off his genius, she's not sure which. And now she's not even going to do them credit when she shows up to accept their accolades and has no real idea where on Earth they came from. She's afraid of failing them, failing him . . .

She goes on for a while, a real gut spilling. That's what she supposes prayer to be, being largely unfamiliar with the process. Her hands and face are wet and snotty. She's tempted to go inside and clean up but doesn't want to cross the threshold again, especially now that she's purged herself. She's not sure if she feels more or less crazy to have spilled her guts like that, but she does feel better. Sort of.

The mountains, the meadows, even the meandering trails forgive her, but there's not a murmur from the man in her heart where she listens for him, where she waits willingly for his judgment, for a word, a touch.

Nothing.

She'll have to face this one on her own, confess to the world what she's done, give it all back, and suffer the consequences. She might even be able to pass it off as an elaborate ruse to validate Sandy's genius. She's not sure, however, if she's good enough to do the right thing. If she were that good and true, she never would have dreamed up the hor- rible thing she's done in the first place, now would she? Now here she is, prizes in hand. She's won the fucking lottery of her dreams. Does she have a "no thank you" in her? She's not sure. She feels like Claudius asking to be forgiven for his brother's murder while he's still screwing the man's wife and sitting on his throne. Not exactly like that, but in the same unforgivable neighborhood. Question is, can she stand to live there on a permanent basis? Live a lie, as they say.

She rises and turns, and there he is, Wilkerson, looking like his midcareer white-haired author photo, a few years younger than the photo on the *Wilkerson Studies* office wall, his face a tanned eroded plain, incredibly handsome, intense, perhaps a little high on something, a wry enigmatic smile. He's dressed in jeans and a battered leather jacket, a dark turtleneck, the uniform of those days. He would later lose the leather jacket.

"Don't worry, I'm dead. I won't tell anyone how naughty you've been and spoil your fun." It's his voice all right, a velvety baritone that made you turn up the radio wondering *who is that man?* He was the darling of NPR. Genevieve has listened to endless hours in the DC archives of his flirtatious banter with one breathless interviewer after another. She got hot just listening. He had an affair with at least one of them, according to the woman's husband who wrote Sandy a series of angry emails, and Sandy's third wife who did a nasty tell-all ghosted bio to coincide with Sandy's fifth marriage. Insufficient evidence you might say until you listen to the unedited interview. "Get a room," you want to say. Apparently, they did.

Genevieve would've expected a ghost to be blurrier or glowier or something. He seems pretty solid. She doesn't find this comforting. "I'm a thieving little cunt," she manages to say in a shaky whisper, just so he'll know what she thought was the most important part of what she was just blathering on about. Somehow she knows he heard it all, that he was listening from the beginning, may have even watched her steal his words away last fall. Sometimes it feels like he's haunted half her life—in her head. This isn't the first time she's spoken to him, though it's the first time he's shown up and spoken back. The first time she's seen him with her eyes wide open. She's trembling all over, from crying, from fear, excitement, she's not sure which.

"Such language," he says. "Such precise language. I approve. We'll have to work on that mouth if you're going to charm anyone, however. Don't be afraid of me, lovely one. I'm always delighted to meet a fan." He smiles at her and waits for her to manage a faint smile back, to try breathing like a normal person. "That's better. So where do we go first to reap these ill-gotten gains you described, accept our accolades? I've missed traveling, being fussed over as far as that goes. Don't worry. No one can see me but you."

"Are— are you real?"

"Little late to be asking that, isn't it? So deep into the proceedings?" He's standing close to her. He reaches out and touches her cheek with the backs of his pale slender fingers, and she shudders and shivers. They're deathly cold. He pulls them away. "You see the problem. It's cold up here on the mountain and getting colder. Make me famous again, little thief. I rather enjoyed it the first time, for a while at least. Never lasts, but what does? You can make all my mistakes and a few of your own. I'll just go along for the ride. I've had sufficient peace and quiet to last me an age."

It's Wilkerson all right. Going along for the ride is a way of life for his characters, for him as well, until he stopped one day here for some reason and wrote brooding poems and narcissistic essays, like the world didn't have enough of those. And seemed to quit what had made him famous; only he didn't, as only she knows. He wrote the novels he wasn't supposed to write but then lost his nerve and stuck them away in the attic. Now, here he is, the man she's betrayed, demanding only to share in the fruits of her sins. She feels like Mary Magdalene that morning in the Garden if Jesus had asked to hitch a ride back into town for a pub crawl—the wine on Him. She knows better than to argue with a dead man, certainly not one she's long adored.

He gets in the passenger seat without opening the door but then plucks a pencil from the junk in the door pocket, stabs the window button and rolls it all the way down. The twisty road out of his place doesn't afford many opportunities for Genevieve to glance at her passenger, but it's definitely him—long, lean, and fit, fortyish plus? It's not quite true that he never aged, but he did it well. Or maybe this is some idealized vision of her fevered brain, a psychotic break with reality of disturbing intensity. A guilt-induced meltdown.

For now, at least, she'd rather be haunted than crazy. Even dead, he's sexy.

He seems absorbed with motion as they make the drive, swaying with the curves and grinning. He sticks his head out of the window like a dog and lets the wind stream through his hair. After a while she tells him she's getting too cold and rolls his window up with her button.

"So, what did you think of them?" he asks her after they've snaked through a half-dozen curves in silence.

She knows he means the novels in the attic. She would've thought her feelings were clear enough in all she said in her porch confession, but apparently not. "I love them," she says. "All of them." She tells him *The Mad Statue* is her favorite, and he smiles—sexy, knowing, mysterious.

"Makes sense," he says. "I abandoned them, like you said. I'd just had an awful fight with my brother. I decided they were all crap. Not as I was writing them, but when it came down to showing them to anybody, I couldn't do it, believe in them enough to risk rejection, a critically acclaimed asshole like myself. I could hear them. *Science Fiction,*

Detectives, Romance, Sandy, really? Have you forgotten who you are? That was the plan, actually, to forget who I was and become someone new. That's what writing fucking novels is always about, for me at least. But when you found them, carried them off, I thought, oh Lord, here it comes, Judgment Day, a coward even in death, but this works out marvelously well. Thanks for the guts, courage, whatever it took. Just tell everybody you learned every fucking thing you know from Sandy Wilkerson, you got it?"

"It's true." About novels. About life. About seizing the moment. About desire.

"Save it for the interviewers. Get an agent, by the way. Immediately. I'd suggest someone, but they're all dead. Don't worry so much about what you're going to say. When asked about what you're working on, always say discussing work-in-progress interferes with your creative process, but you're very excited about how it's going."

"But I'm not working on anything. Everything *I've* ever written is crap."

"I was forgetting what an honorable soul you are, suggesting you lie." He laughs heartily. He looks over at her quite fondly, like she's imagined him doing so many times in fantasies. "It's okay, really, what you did. I don't know why I left those manuscripts up there. I'd deleted them all from everything, tired of worrying about revising them again— as if they would ever please me—but I couldn't destroy the printed pages, a silly ritual to celebrate the supposed end. A printing, a drink, a celebration, the beginning of regret. I couldn't destroy them twice. Shredded, you say? I didn't have one of those. I would've had to haul them out of the attic, feed them into the fire, page by page. Didn't much like the symbolism in that. Genius resurrected by devoted acolyte seems much preferable to me. Just be brave and charming, young and pretty, smart as hell—be yourself in other words. They've already given you the prizes. They're not likely to take them back. You deserve them, my darling. You've made a dead man happy, no easy task."

***

He's excited by the city, a little stunned at the sprawl, but delighted otherwise by the changes he sees since he was here last twenty-two years ago. As they cross over the river, he's beaming. "So, they didn't fuck it up."

When they get home—technically Clint's place where she's now all but moved in—just like Sandy said, Clint can't see him, and Wilkerson blows her a kiss, wanders off somewhere to visit old haunts, exiting through the south wall as Clint is trying to show her the exciting bits he's discovered in the pile of travel books on the table for her prize claiming itinerary. He's almost as excited by all this as she is, though her attention has shifted from her adopted children to their father.

She just rode into town with the ghost of Sandy Wilkerson. How beyond wildest dreams is that? It's *Casablanca* is what it is. Only her true love's not married to a freedom fighter, he's dead. She always cries at the end of *Casablanca*.

Clint's made spaghetti and meatballs, and she starts to tell Clint a thousand times over dinner, "I rode home with Sandy," but knows he'd only think her crazy. She's not an Ancient Mariner. She's his girlfriend. He likes ghost stories because he doesn't believe in them. They spend all evening making plans for her award-winning future. Clint goes to bed exhausted; she promises to follow soon, saying she has a lot to think about.

More like one huge thing.

***

Sandy shows up as she's washing the dishes. He helps himself to the last of the wine Clint bought to celebrate, three times what they would usually spend on a bottle. "I like Clint," he tells her. "Seems crazy about you."

"He's true," she tells him. She doesn't like the way it comes out.

Sandy stands at the counter beside her, close. "I can see that. Question is, are you?" He plucks a cold meatball Clint left beached on the plate and pops it in his mouth, chews with obvious relish. Ghosts have appetites apparently. She could never do that, leave a meatball on the plate. She washes the plate, puts it in the rack.

"I hoped you'd come back," Sandy says. "I loved having you there, moving through the place, walking the trails, sleeping in my bed. Almost three years, isn't it."

She nods her head.

He doesn't mention her masturbating in the meadow re-enacting scenes from his novels in her head and loins. He's standing behind her now, very close, his hands on the counter on either side of her. She recalls her lengthy confession was quite explicit about her adolescent feelings for him. She didn't give an end date for those feelings.

"Really?" she asks, looking over her shoulder, turning her face to him.

His right arm wraps around her waist, his cold left hand caresses her cheek as he kisses her full on the mouth. His cold tongue grows warm twining with hers. His cold fingers lose their chill buried in her hair. He tastes of meatball. Their bodies grind together. Her breath is hot enough for both of them. His right hand slips beneath her shirt and squeezes her left breast, and she groans like a statue coming to life and accidentally kicks the cabinet. She unzips her jeans, and guides his hand down—

51

There's a sound in the hall, Clint in the doorway. She doesn't get to find out if ghosts fuck, but has the distinct impression, lingering sensation—stiff ghost cock nestled firmly in the crack of her ass—that they do.

And she would.

"Were you talking to someone?" Clint asks, drowsy and confused, at sea. He's not wearing his glasses. The world is a ghostly blur.

"I was just practicing my acceptance speeches," she says, laughing at herself, wiping a dab of tomato sauce from the corner of her mouth, zipping up her jeans, trying to slow her breathing. She knocks back the last of the wine. Maybe that's it. The expensive wine. Her system just can't handle it.

He goes back to bed, and she soon follows, hoping she'll be safe there. Surely Sandy won't show up with Clint lying next to her. The man's been married *five* times, she reminds herself. *And* he's dead. Stone cold dead. Though he does warm quickly.

***

She rereads, as she often does, the opening chapter of *The Mad Statue*. She's glad in a way that out of all of them it didn't win, that it's still hers alone for now, her and her passionate ghost's.

Chapter One: Mirth Awakes

Some statues awaken and perceive the world around them, become aware. It only stands to reason. Stand motionless long enough, and anything begins to sound reasonable.

This particular statue is staring, was staring, had been staring, would be staring. Staring, staring, staring—at a point just below the riverbank, so she can't see the river except when there's an exceptional flood every twenty years or so, and then she only catches glimpses of the brown, frothy, sluggish skirts of it, listening to the chatter of the people who've come down here special to see the river, admire its beauty and its power. People don't all love each other in Richmond, but they all love the river.

She stands on a hillside, once part of a rich man's estate, now a city park. She's a Victorian copy of an Antonio Canova marble and has an exceptionally nice ass. Many hands have touched her nice marble ass. Maybe one of them was magic and awakened her. She knows whatever they knew, the ones who touch her, which makes her think the magic came from the sculptor who made her, the first one to fondle her perfect ass. His idea of perfection too, she's guessing. It's nice to have a creator, somebody who loves you, but you know how artists are, they just might hate you too—see you as a mistake, a sellout, a who knows what all. But at one time he poured himself into me, even if I was only a copy.

I'm the statue in question, your narrator.

No use maintaining that narrative third person façade, but it's what we're used to as statues—we *mean* something first, then have a nice ass or interesting face later, when, just like people, sometimes I wish for the other way around. I'm Mirth. Nice to meet you.

I figure a good god, sculptor, whatever ought to stick with his creation. Not like the cowardly Dr. Frankenstein. A celebratory graduate student who had just defended her thesis on Frankenstein's Creature, whom she adored beyond all reason—like the mate Frankenstein never made him—told me all this as she lay her hand on my ass, because it reminded her of a lover's ass who wasn't there to celebrate her defense, but was somewhere else with some other woman.

I can understand more than you might think. As much as he loved me, my maker sold me to the rich people who used to live here, and I never saw him again. That's what it means to be art, even a copy like me. It gets you out in the world. That's both good and bad.

I'm Mirth, one of the Three Graces. Something's happened to my sisters, Splendor and Good Cheer, who used to flank me. I don't know what exactly, but could hear the blows, feel the tremors. I couldn't turn to see. Graceless Vandals in the night with picks and sledgehammers. I was to be next, when they were frightened off by Security.

Maybe that's why I've gone mad. Whatever the reason, I've about had it with this hillside, this still point I stare at *like a statue*, which is precisely why most statues who awaken decide it's a very bad idea and go right back to being the blockheads their makers intended them to be before they die of boredom.

I've been awake for decades.

I don't want to sleep until I see the river. Is that too much to ask? I didn't stand here all this time to never see her. I listen to her all day and all night. Always constant, but always changing. I'm constant, but I'm stone, and stone can crumble, erode, crack, and shatter—not exactly the sort of change one longs for. I thought I had my chance a few years ago when an earthquake shook the park, and I hoped for a new perspective, but we didn't budge, staring at the same spot since that big oak was a sapling. I love that oak, I truly do, but I long to see flow, to let current course through my thighs.

This thought seeped into my mind through a tiny fissure in the crown of my lovely head during a long, wet summer when the waters were particularly noisome and thought provoking, and a horny lonely philosophy major had just fondled my ass, recalling the last time she stood in the river with the woman she misses—the woman who loves Frankenstein's Creature. Magic attracts magic, and I'm as magic as it gets just talking to you, telling my own story.

As if losing my sisters isn't bad enough, Security is surrounding me with iron bars—like a jail. No one will ever touch me again.

The park workers just want to keep me safe, though they can't resist a parting fondle when the welding's done. They all agree it's a shame, a waste. One declares I have the most beautiful ass he's ever seen in his life.

His companions laugh at the foolishness of his choice, but not at his taste. They all agree, however, that beauty isn't everything, and flesh is preferable to stone. They all have wives and girlfriends back home they long to touch. Their fading laughter makes me feel like a spurned lover, abandoned in a walled garden. Eve with no Adam.

Alone.

God's very condition when the universe began. Never underestimate the power of loneliness. Maybe that's the feeling that finally does it for me, dissolves a few molecules or stretches their bonds or whatever so that my head tilts back a few degrees, and I see the river at last, look into the heart of it.

So this is flow. My Goddess! Would you look at that?

Once I have the knack of it—flow—I find my limbs are as supple and flexible as they look. The river taught me all that with just one glance.

"You ain't seen nothing yet," the river calls to me. "You don't know a thing about mirth until you've been with me." The river is Motion. The river is Life. The river knows what she's talking about. She beckons.

I dissolve the bonds, free myself from the sad remnants of my sisters, step down from the pedestal, crushing the newly constructed fence, and slide down the hillside into the shallows. I stand in the river, water gushing around my lovely legs, turn my supple waist and survey my new domain upstream and down and feel it, really feel it, for the first time from the inside out: Mirth! I burst—a first—into joyous laughter. I have a beautiful laugh.

"*That's* what I'm talking about," the river says. As everyone from crazed evangelist to skinny-dipping teen understands, there's no *maybe* about the river's magic.

In a statue, I suppose, any laughter is madness, even a titter. Mad I must be. I dive beneath the waves, surface, and scramble onto a sister rock, tagged here and there by revelers and idealists. I've discovered my passion, a mission to spread the word. I've thought about it hard and long. A statue should stand for something, or what's a statue for? I'll awaken my fellow statues so they can experience this bliss and *move*. Not just to stand for something, but to live it in the world, in the flow. I knew it would feel good—many lives have touched me—I thought I knew a thing or two—I've had decades to weigh this life and that—but *this* good? No way. Mirth. The real thing.

Where to start? Richmond's full of statues, full of meanings. Some must be fairly forlorn if they've had the misfortune to awaken and not be free, and those who slumber might like to know what they mean now and have a chance to step out and look around. Live. Pygmalion was one of my creator's favorite stories—not unusual in sculptors I would imagine.

I sniff the air for some solid notion and catch a whiff of Columbus to the north. Discovery and Conquest, the myth of *El Nuevo Mundo*—a delicious fantasy. Poor Chris has been staring at a park lake full of pedal boats. It's time he discovered the undiscovered country the other side of the downtown expressway where he's never gone before. I know my way around. There was a bus driver who couldn't pass me by without a caress.

I know Columbus's story. I feel like Queen Isabel. Not like the Servant of God who booted the Jews, but the other one who financed that bold visionary who had no idea where he was going and didn't know where he was when he got there, Christopher Columbus, discoverer of a place that was there all along. Who knew besides the thousands of folks who lived there? Maybe he can finally find the place he was searching for if I awaken him. The New World. The creation of a multitude of hands . . .

Chapter Five

The Dance

A Real Agent

O body swayed to music, O brightening glance,
How can we know the dancer from the dance?
                    —*William Butler Yeats, "Among School Children"*

Andy, the nice man who called to tell Genevieve she'd won for
Sandstorm asked if she had an agent. When she said she didn't, he
strongly suggested one might be useful and gave her the name and number of his. Andy, a dear, sweet man, was one of the judges. He gushed
about the book in a way that made her uncomfortable. She didn't understand half of what he was saying, especially when he talked about
how the book riffed off other science fiction. Genevieve has never read
any science fiction because Sandy once said it was all crap, and one
branch of literature you can safely ignore in the halls of academe is science fiction. She'll have to ask Sandy why he changed his mind—or
convinced Andy he did—and to give her a reading list.

An agent, however, sounds like a good idea. Sandy seemed quite
certain about it. Genevieve figures if a real writer like Sandy thought
he needed an agent, a phony like her needs one even more—since she
didn't really do what she's claimed to have done, she doesn't know what
she's doing, and she has no idea at all what to do next. Maybe she needs
a guide dog. Sandy loved dogs. Genevieve had the experience only

briefly. When Dad left, he took the dog, Barney, with him. After that, her mother had a word for dogs: No. If she's going to be hanging out with Sandy, maybe she should get a dog. One of the poets had a dog, a whip-smart border collie. Genevieve was crazy about that dog, the poet not so much.

She calls the agent's number, drops Andy's name. Agent's name is Roberta Stone, and Genevieve doesn't think she's all that interested until she rattles off the names of the contests in which she's won or placed.

"Hold on. So, let me get this straight. You won or were runner-up for a literary novel—something avant-garde I'm guessing—a romance, a private eye mystery, a science fiction novel—all at the same time? What have you been doing with them? You couldn't have written them all at once."

Genevieve explains how she never thought her work good enough, that she was the victim of her own high standards, but when she turned thirty, she decided to take a chance and submit the five, albeit under five pseudonyms. She's actually 27, but she *feels* thirty. All those years as Bent's girl, barely escaping a scholarly spinsterhood, have left their mark. She feels like Dorothea must've when she was finally shed of Casaubon. *Middlemarch* was a Sandy favorite.

"Just as well," Roberta says. "We may want to keep your genre identities separate for now. They don't always get along. Send me the prizewinners and the runners-up. Hold off on the crazy statue book for now. That sounds a little creepy. Off-market. Maybe later, when you're more established."

"It's my favorite."

"The author's judgment often isn't the most reliable measure in my experience."

What about a thief's? Don't they usually know the value of the swag?

"What are you working on now?" Roberta asks.

Nothing but holding it together just barely, but Genevieve remembers Sandy's advice. "I find that discussing work in progress interferes with my creative process, but it's going well. I'm quite pleased, actually."

"Damn. You're one of those?"

"That's right. One of those."

"What about a genre?"

"What about it?"

"What *genre* is this thing that's going so well?"

"Does it matter?"

"Of course, it matters."

"Interesting."

"Okay, I get it. No discussing the work. You're going to accept the prizes, I hope."

"I planned to. Should I go to the runners-up things too?"

"Absolutely. Be gracious. Be nicer than the winner. When the winner gets too drunk to schmooze, move into the vacuum. Which one's first?"

"The Clute-Wolfe Prize for Fresh Fantastika. It's in Florida in a few months."

"I know. I'll be there. How well do you know the genre?"

"Sci-fi?"

Was that a groan? "I see. Never say sci-fi, understand? It's complicated. What science fiction have you read?"

"*Frankenstein*, that's science fiction, right? I love that book. *1984*."

"*Brave New World*. Right. Look. I could accept for you, as your agent. Create an aura of mystery, you know? Like Pynchon."

"I wouldn't miss it. There's a banquet, right? They make a big fuss. You just said I should go." Part of her understanding with Sandy is if she's going to do the famous writer thing, she's to do it all—and bring him along. He wants to hear the applause, sip the wine. He was lonely long before he was a ghost. "Don't worry," Genevieve purrs in her best Texas accent. "I know how to bull shit."

Roberta laughs. "You did say you're from Texas. Just don't say sci-fi. Say science fiction. Even better, say 'the fantastic'. Can you say that for me?"

"The Fantastic." Genevieve's been in lit crit long enough to know the importance of a good term, and she says it with feeling, hitting the second syllable hard, ready to defend whatever wonky notions it's supposed to embody, as if a word could embody anything.

"Beautiful," Roberta says. "You'll do great. I'll get back to you when I've read them."

***

Genevieve stands in the kitchen, looking out the window into the park, listening to the radio. There's a lake with ducks and geese, kids feeding them Wonder Bread even though they shouldn't. She'll curse them later when she walks through all the goose shit, but right now they make her smile. *I have a motherfucking AGENT!* What all her MFA boyfriends would call a "Real Agent." Imposters were rife apparently.

One of the best things about living with Clint is the windows. Her place is a windowless basement cave, chosen more than six years ago, she recalls, so she wouldn't be tempted to linger there too long. The radio's playing a medley of Strauss waltzes, and she's thinking about *2001: A Space Odyssey* and science fiction. Does it matter that we've passed that future right by? She likes that. It makes you think about what time is, space. We make it up as we go along. That's why she likes *The Mad Statue* so much. Anything can happen. The past won't rest, the future beckons. Mirth and madness rule: *I have a Literary Agent even though I've never written anything but a few steaming piles eviscerated on the workshop table!*

It's like one of those make-a-wish stories in which you don't ask for just the right thing and fuck the whole thing up. She should've asked for talent, but all she asked for was success. Be careful what you wish for.

Sandy shows up in the middle of this reverie, so she asks him what he meant when he said it made sense *The Mad Statue* is her favorite.

"You long to break free."

"From what?"

"Does it matter?" He looks into her eyes. Apparently, he means to take up where they left off. Even dead, his eyes are a deep sky blue.

"Don't," she says and steps back, but he steps with her, puts a hand to her waist, another to her elbow and dances to the music. She follows, of course she follows. It's not their first dance. There's a dance scene in *Don't* she first imagined with him when she didn't know he was dead. He looked younger on that book jacket, but she still had to tell him that the difference in their ages didn't matter to her in the least. He was a passionate, tender, and considerate lover in her imagination. Sometimes before, sometimes after, they'd dance, though this is their first waltz. They were mostly into tangos and Texas bar music in those days.

Dead's a whole other question.

He holds her close as they circle around the kitchen, whirling more times than she would've thought possible in such a small kitchen. It helps she's not wearing a Strauss appropriate skirt. It's delicious. It's been a long time. She adjusts to the cold, or perhaps she warms him. He's a terrific dancer, gives her the illusion she's one too, a delusion dead for a decade. She closes her eyes and surrenders until the end of the waltz, when he whispers, his lips to her ear, "Congrats on your agent.

Now all your old boyfriends can hate you. Don't be afraid, little thief, I won't hurt you. I'll be the perfect stranger."

He kisses her cheek, and he's gone, and she's shivering cold, her arms wrapped tight around herself, and she wants to cry out for him to wait, to come back, but she's shivering too hard to speak, to form words. She scurries down the hall into the bathroom and turns on the hot water in the shower. When the steam clouds start to rise, she strips off her clothes and stands under the scalding water until she stops shaking, until she feels cooked down to her toes, but she can still feel his embrace.

Willingly.

She's the forger in this story, stealing someone else's art, but unlike Dante in *Willingly*, she's taking credit for it, not just the money but the accolades. Genevieve never thought her name and "accolades" would ever inhabit the same sentence. Dante's problem is he falls in love with the model he chose in the first place only because she looks like the real artist's favorite model. He can't get too close to her. He never lets her see the painting, so she can't rat him out prematurely when he says Famous Painter did it and fools the Art World, a favorite enemy of many a hapless artist. His payoff, when he reveals himself as the forger, is to make the expert arbiters of taste eat crow. He's in it strictly for the rebellion, which is basically why the novel was written, a fuck you to whatever forces didn't want Sandy to write it. He clearly had fun writing it. You can tell. Or she can anyway. She knows him better than she knows herself, though that's setting the bar fairly low. In the end, the model, who reminds Genevieve more than a little of herself, lies to save Dante from the law, and they live happily ever after.

She's headed straight for an affair with a ghost, a dead man. But not just any zombie. Her favorite dead man of all time. For half her life now, she's resurrected him in every way imaginable short of magic elixir—and confided in him, questioned him, laughed with him, fucked

him, cried on his shoulder because she couldn't, not really, and that was
the saddest thing in the world in a generally sad world as it was, but
somehow that made her happy, kept her sane, if you accept that she is.
And now here he is, walking through her door, any door. She couldn't
lock him out if she wanted to.

Maybe she should be on meds for this. What kind of shit do they
give you to keep you from seeing a dead man—and talking with him
and dancing with him and fucking him like you've spent half your life
imagining in one way or another? Though now it's not a fantasy; it's
real. Or at least that's the way it feels. Would she take such a drug if
she had it?

***

She forgot to ask him how he came to write a sci-f—a science fiction
novel, after saying such nasty things about the genre. No matter. She
likes *Sandstorm*; they liked *Sandstorm* well enough to give it a prize.
All she has to do is show up and not be a total idiot. So, she has some
reading to do. Roberta suggested some online magazines where she
might address her sf illiteracy. ("SF is okay?" Genevieve asked; "usually," Roberta replied.)

Swaddled in flannel pajamas and wool socks and some garish assemblage of granny squares crocheted somewhere in Clint's past by a
great aunt Lu, she searches the web for science fiction to see what she
can read for free. What better place to look? She starts by searching
stories by the former winners of the prize she just won. Soon she's into
multiple issues of *Lightspeed, Clarkesworld, Strange Horizons, Apex,*
and *Subterranean*. She fucking loves it. The guy who brutalized her
fiction in his workshop hated sci-fi, as he called it too, never without a
sneer. Genevieve is beginning to understand why the term might grate.

When Clint comes home and finds her, he asks why she's bundled up when it's in the seventies. She's not sick, is she?

Sweet Clint. Define sick. She holds up her tablet. "I was on a frozen planet. I'm doing some research for Florida. Science fiction stories. Very cool stuff. I think I'm a fan. I got an agent."

She warms to the subject of Roberta to distract herself and Clint both from chillier matters, and soon she's shrugged off the crocheted throw, a riot of bright yarns, remnants Clint explained once, from other projects. Aunt Luella couldn't let anything go to waste.

Makes sense, Genevieve reasons, it's a harsh and lonely planet sometimes, a featureless plain, a stagnant sea. You have to recycle. You take your scraps of color and warmth where you can find them or make them up. She likes visiting imagined worlds. It reminds her how much we make up this one.

"I'm so happy for you," he says, but what does he mean? *I'm so glad you're getting away with it?* She's not sure how she feels about that. The long-term effects of the complete confession, she knows from more than one Wilkerson novel, aren't always rosy. Though now her confession's hardly complete, is it?— having omitted the small detail of another man wooing her, much less that the man is the dead author of the purloined tomes, for whom she has burned almost as long as that limbic pilot light's been lit. *I stole his books—he stole my heart!* Too much? Heart? is that what we're talking about here?

She hugs Clint. His warm, comfortable arms wrap around her. The man knows what an albatross-shooting bitch needs at such moments. Warmth. Not forgiveness. He thinks he doesn't have to forgive her because he loves her. She's not so sure of that. Since she hasn't forgiven herself, his forgiveness would be premature. It just doesn't matter to him. That's its own forgiveness of a sort. Or maybe like his Aunt Lu, he can't throw anything away. You weave it back together one way or another, make the pieces fit. Then give it to your student nephew. For whatever reason, he seems almost as invested in the success of the novels as she is.

***

You remember how Genevieve's mom discovered her in a compromising position with Scissorhands? This has established an almost magical pattern in Genevieve's life: At every sexual crossroads, there's Mom. Contemplating fucking the dead, for example? Genevieve's not surprised when her phone rings, and it's Mom. At the Greyhound station, come for a short visit. Should she get a cab, or can Genevieve pick her up? Mom's not much of a planner, doesn't like to telegraph her goofiness. Mom says she just had to get the fuck out of Texas.

Genevieve can relate.

She hasn't told her mother about her stupendous success as an author yet because lying to your mother, as common as it is, seems like an especially bad thing to do. She talks the question over with Clint as he's racing around to get to class, obviously still processing that his girlfriend's mom—the wild one he's been hearing about for months now—is showing up indefinitely, and he says it's her call whether to tell Mom the whole truth or not, that he can see the sense in either way, etc., etc., then he's gone.

That's the trouble with an intellectual boyfriend. Too reasonable. You pose a problem; you get an analysis, a précis. No help at all when you need a gut check. It's like asking him, just what the fuck *does* that albatross mean? Who has time for the answer? And in the end, you'd be more confused than ever. When who cares? Be your own damn albatross.

Sandy's waiting in the car when she goes to get Mom. "I don't have time for any of your nonsense right now. You're dead, for Christ's sake, and my fucking mother's waiting at the bus station." She tries not to whine, but there it is, unmistakable, like a screeching windshield wiper.

"You underestimate me," he says. "I heard your crisis and am offering my advice, since the Professor, dear boy, couldn't possibly: Tell her. She'll know her baby girl didn't write five novels and hide them away. You might be clever enough, but way too cheeky not to brag about them. She won't rat you out, will she? Your own Mum?"

"Rat me out? No. You don't have to put it like that."

"How would you like me to put it, my darling?"

"Don't call me darling. It's not going to happen, okay? You're dead. Get over it. Nobody says 'my darling' anymore anyway."

"Pity. Suits you. As you wish. You going to tell her the truth?'

"Yeah."

"You going to tell her about me?"

Somewhere in this discussion his hand has ended up on her thigh. She lays her hand on his. The last time she touched his hand was to encourage it; this time she means to halt any further progress. It's cold. "You should wear gloves," she suggests. "Do you think I should tell her about you?"

"That I'm a ghost, or I'm your lover?"

"We're *not* lovers."

"Fair enough," he says and looks into her eyes. She grips his hand and squeezes. He squeezes her thigh and is gone. She sticks her hand under her butt to warm it, and her cheek turns cold through the denim like she's sitting on a block of ice. She sighs and half expects to see a frosty cloud. *I see dead people.* One person anyway, one too many. Is that why her heart is racing? Doesn't feel like fear or anger.

She flies down the Boulevard to the bus station like the Mad Statue on a mission, passing under Stonewall's shadow. She glances in the rearview as if he might be following her. This is getting too weird to handle.

Fortunately she doesn't have to decide right away what to tell Mom because Mom's full of tales of BJ, her most recent soon-to-be-ex, who has turned out to be a totally worthless son of a bitch, as Genevieve always figured he had to be if Mom chose him. Not another dentist seems to be the only requirement she makes of each new loser. All Genevieve has to do to keep the conversation going is ask what Mom did next after suffering one outrage after another. It brings back memories, other men, other monologues. To Mom's credit, none of them were ever mean, just useless.

By the time Genevieve's gotten Mom home and fed her lunch, Mom's just made it to the part where BJ's quit going to AA *again*, and Genevieve's ready to scream out her own horrid story just to get Mom to shut the fuck up. Sandy's right. She has to tell her. If only to change the subject.

Fortunately, Clint comes home and charms Mom with his young professor schtick.

"Call me Ella," she says and giggles.

And he does. "Has Genevieve told you her big news, Ella?"

Clint means the prizes, of course, the Good News. He seems to have assumed Genevieve would lie to her own mother and Mom doesn't know the worst—the Truth. "Why don't you tell her?" Genevieve suggests. Let him handle the exposition, then she can make her confession.

Clint never sits down, like he's still in front of a class. He's totally excited by the accomplishments of Ella's girl, Genevieve. He quotes from some of the flattering official notification letters, like he's forgetting she stole her winners, like he really believes she wrote them somehow. She feels this thing slipping out of her control again as she watches her mother's face infuse with pride, not an immediately recognizable look from a mom who used to plead with her daughter to "at *least* make an attempt not to be so fucking weird" because she read all the time. And this is in the middle of a tale of Mom's own personal man troubles. Mom usually hates to be blown off course. Mom was totally open minded. You could tell her *anything*. You want to be a nun? A serial killer? That's wonderful, dear, just don't go *on* about it. Don't ask me to care. Let me finish saying what I was saying before you interrupted me, so you'll know that whatever you said, it means nothing to me.

And yet, somehow, when the tale is being told by cute Clint, she can't get enough of it.

Mom throws her arms around her only child and confirms the impossible, "Genevieve, I'm so proud of you! I always knew you were special. Always, always, always!"

Mom gets a little weepy. That and the beer with lunch, and the long bus ride, soon send her to bed. Clint holes up to read student essays. That leaves Genevieve alone in the living room with Sandy. "That went well," he says.

"Oh fuck you," she says.

He smiles at the suggestion. "You should have Clint do all the talking. He's already enjoying your fame. It's very sweet. One would almost think he doesn't know you stole them."

"I thought you forgave me for that."

"That doesn't mean I want you to forget it."

"Don't worry. Do you still think I should tell Mom the truth?"

"No need now that she's swallowed the whole thing. She must have had a great hunger for good news. Were you a disappointing child, Genevieve?"

"Is the plan to provoke me until I leap on you in a fury, and my rage turns to ravenous lust in your powerful arms?" There's more than one scene that goes like that in his novels, scenes she's reread with guilty pleasure.

"Would that work?"

"Doubtful."

"You're lying, I can tell, but I don't want to rush you into anything. We have a long road ahead. Wouldn't want to miss all the banquets and things. We can always get to the ravenous lust later."

"I never know when you're serious."

"I'm never serious. Though dead's rather serious, I suppose. Casts a pall, as they say."

She laughs. Laughter in the midst of pathos, a Wilkerson trademark. "So why did you write a science fiction novel when you said all those nasty things about the genre?"

"I wanted to write about change. Not just the personal epiphany bits, but more. Things can always be otherwise. I said all those stupid things about the genre because I got into a drunken argument with an asshole who thought he was smarter than me."

Couldn't have that. Genevieve knows the very asshole, has read the accounts of the incident, but discreetly leaves him nameless. "*Was* he smarter?"

"Of course. Why else would I say such stupid things? I hadn't read any science fiction. It was effortless to detest it. In those days, your dislikes were a measure of your worth, the more things you hated, the better you were. Science fiction was an easy target, like picking on a homeless derelict. Interviewers would egg me on, dredge it up, looking for me to say something nastier than last time."

"When they weren't flirting with you."

"Is that jealousy?" He laughs warmly. "How nice. Don't worry my d—Genevieve, now I'm yours alone."

"I alone can see you?"

"That's right."

"People would call me crazy."

"All the more reason not to let such rude folk see me."

Reportedly, Genevieve recalls, the other man took a swing, though she could never track down confirmation that it connected or what Sandy did then. When asked in later years, he always declined to comment.

As for the interviewers, he led them on. Charmed the pants right off of them, as Mom would say.

***

She's still weighing her options here as she understands them—haunted or batshit—when Mom emerges bleary-eyed and needs coffee brewed. "Nice place," Mom says, looking out the same window Genevieve looked out pondering *2001* before her magical waltz with Sandy. Now it's *All Things Considered*.

Genevieve shuts it off. They never live up to their name. Not a word about ghost lovers, for example. You have to go to old ballads for that—one of Genevieve's favorite genres. Murder ballads were the soundtrack of her adolescence.

"I've always wanted to go to Florida," Mom says.

Oh shit. Genevieve considers asking a few follow-ups about BJ to distract her from this terrible idea. (His name's Robert Joseph, Bob-Joe, Bojo, BJ—Mom uses them all). You can bet there's hours and hours more to tell. Nothing's worth that. "Would you like to go to Florida with us, Mom?"

It's the guilt. She knows it is. If this was the Middle Ages, Genevieve might have beaten herself with a scourge to atone for past sins and sins to come. Now she merely has to invite Mom along to share in the realization of her dreams. Genevieve is grateful to be living in a more subtle age.

She calls Andy, and he sounds delighted to add Mom to her party. Is there anyone else besides boyfriend and Mom? Dead author perhaps? Sandy assures her he'll be there, that he'll manage to be at her side, wherever she goes, whenever she needs him. One of the perks of being dead, apparently, is easy travel. Madness too, she supposes, stays on your trail wither thou wander.

***

Roberta calls late. She's wound up. Genevieve is sitting up in bed reading a terrific Jeffrey Ford story while Clint sleeps beside her. "I read them all. All terrific. New strategy: I'm pitching them as a package deal to big houses that cover the genres—one home for all of them—all under one name. Your name or one of the pseudonyms. You have a preference?"

"Mine, I guess."

"Great. I'll get them out there in the morning. We want a quick answer so we can get the edits done and put ARCs in people's hands before the awards ceremonies."

"ARCs?"

"Advanced Reading Copies."

"Oh. Like books, for reviews."

"Exactly. I'm also pursuing film options simultaneously."

"Film options. Simultaneously."

"Yes. There's an agent I work with in Hollywood. He can't wait to see them. Any questions?"

Will I burn in Hell for this? "Not—not that I can think of."

"Great. I'll keep you posted. I'm setting up an auction. Talk to you soon."

Genevieve feels the room spinning. She slips out of bed, staggering a little as she makes her way through the dark to find Sandy and tell him the news: They're going to be a sensation. Clint continues to sleep.

Chapter Six

The Fantastic

Proof of Concept

Science fiction is hard to define because it is the literature of change and it changes while you are trying to define it.

—Tom Shippey

Genevieve's been to plenty of these things before, literary conventions of one sort or another, large and small. Most of the ones she's been to, in her role as graduate assistant to an eminent scholar or occasional presenter of a paper of her own, have concerned themselves with mostly dead authors, while this one is focused equally on the living, a few of whom are actually in attendance to witness what is said about them. She, as far as she knows, is the only one who's brought along her favorite dead author to tell her what to say. Scholars and authors seem to be getting on famously. She tries to imagine Sandy sitting through a session on his work without bursting out laughing or strangling someone and smiles at the thought.

He'd actually be a dear, let them have their fun. An interviewer once asked him if it bothers him when his work is misunderstood. He said, "Understanding's over-rated. I just hope not to bore anyone. If I'm meeting someone, I'd much rather be fascinating than understood. Everybody reads their own novel. It's theirs to play in. Misreading isn't possible." In correspondence with those close to him, however, he would sometimes lament being misunderstood, but never in public. He didn't want to make anyone feel stupid. If he wasn't understood, he believed, that was the fault of the fiction not the reader.

***

After she's stowed Mom in her room and Clint's in the shower, Sandy steps through the door to their room without a knock, just a grin, babbling the exciting news that there's an alligator and a hot tub, the former in the small containment pond out back, and the latter adjacent to the indoor pool. He's like a kid, always was, all sixty years as far as she can tell. The stuff he wrote toward the end, she alone knows, was the goofiest of all, but in a good way. He let something go—the hand-some prize winner—let someone loose—The Fool.

They've spent hours together the last few months editing the manu-scripts. She'd expected him to do all that. He was the writer, after all, but he insisted that she do it. They went through all four manuscripts together, discussing each and every editorial suggestion, criticism, de-letion, question. Style and grammar were easy (stet, stet, stet, stet . . .). But the real issues and changes were trickier. He took every editorial word seriously. They argued it out. Sometimes she swore he was play-ing devil's advocate, just so she'd own whatever ended up on the page. Toward the end of the third one—she can be slow—she realized he was teaching her how to write in a sly indirect way. She wanted to make love to him right then and there, but they still had a whole other manu-script to get through—*Willingly*, the romance. The editor wanted the sex hotter. They spent hours on that until it fucking glowed in the dark. She loved every minute of it.

Genevieve updated a few things while she was at it, putting smart phones in characters' hands and getting them out of phone booths, for example, and Sandy approved.

When the boxes of ARCs came Fed-Ex on a bright sunshiny day, it was Sandy she wanted to celebrate with, roaming the locales of their novels, but it was Clint she ate a celebratory al fresco sandwich with, missing Sandy the whole time.

Now here they are. The Sensation's first adventure. Prize One.

Walk the walk time.

Sandy acts like he's on his sixth honeymoon, looks like the cover photo from midway through his career, the one Genevieve pictures when she closes her eyes, the one who displaced Scizzorhands in her erotic evolution, and now here they are in Florida for a long weekend. It's an airport Marriott, like every other Marriott only this one is chock-full of the fantastic for the next few days, and she's hoping some of that magic will rub off on the place. Everyone's being so nice to her, she's already overwhelmed with guilt, and she's only just begun lying her ass off.

Sandy reassures her she's doing wonderfully, using the opportunity to encircle her with his cold embrace. What does it say about her that she finds it comforting? She's sweaty from the steamy Florida air, soon chilled in his arms, her head resting on his chest, listening for his heartbeat. Finding none, she experiences a shudder of a different sort and pushes him away.

"I can't do this," she says.

"Sure you can. Have you decided what to read yet?" He points to the schedule where her prizewinning name appears in bold promising a reading from her honored text tomorrow, followed by a Q & A and signing. There are advanced reader's copies of *Sandstorm* in every registrant's book bag. Lots of reviewers attend this conference. The next day some scholar's going to interview her about her work and her place in the field. On the bench one minute, stealing home the next. On the bench—who is she kidding?—more like bat boy or the kid breaking into cars on the parking lot. She wasn't even in the club. Dad was the baseball fan. He left the sports metaphors behind when he took off.

As terrifying as all that is, that's not the "this" she was talking about. It's the "him this"—fucking a ghost, an old flame, dead from the get-go. She'd read all his stuff and was on the second read when she asked the librarian when there might be another Wilkerson novel, and the librarian said, "Never. He's dead." Like it was no big deal. Genevieve was just shy of fifteen. She started sobbing in the library. But he doesn't know all that, does he? Did he haunt her even then?

"I haven't even thought about it," she says of the reading. She has, but only in relation to the terror of stage fright. She's been carrying around one of the ARCs, but every time she starts to open it, she sees her name on the cover, and she can't get past it, like it's a taboo line. She's delivered papers, speeches, chaired meetings and so forth, all with aplomb, but never anticipated anyone rising in the back of the audience to denounce her as a thief and a fraud. An uninspired, shallow thinker, perhaps, a genuine dullard, possibly, but not a scheming charlatan. Part of her feels like a sexy outlaw, like a Wilkerson heroine. A made-up person.

"Just read the first chapter," Sandy suggests. "So you don't have to set it up. I'll coach you."

"But it isn't *mine*."

"Stop it. Sure it is. You believed in it, fucking resurrected it from the grave. Of course, it's yours. I wrote it for you."

"You didn't even know I was alive."

"No, I didn't, but it's true nonetheless. You think I wrote it for editors, publishers, bookstores, *reviewers*, for Christ's sake? All the rest of that nonsense? The only way I could write those books at all was to write them for the ideal companion who wanted to hear a story, who wanted to be taken away, taken inside another life, taken with me, I suppose."

"The Perfect Stranger."

"Exactly so. I didn't know you were alive, true enough, but I hoped you were—exactly you—and that's better if you think about it, not so creepy. So, I wrote them for you if anyone. A gift. A buffet. Now that you've swallowed them, they're yours. A cook doesn't own the meal he serves once it's eaten, right?"

"You're just being nice."

"No, I'm being fucking profound, confiding the wisdom of the dead, shamelessly mixing metaphors. No one wants your guilt, my darling, but everyone likes a good yarn. Whatever you do, don't read it like you're dead yourself. Anything worth reading is worth seasoning with a good deal of ham. They won't care about its authenticity. Fiction's a pack of lies after all. Pretend! You're good at it. You should write it down, by the way, tell your own stories."

"Tried that. Didn't work out."

"You didn't like it?"

"I wasn't any good. I don't have any talent."

"Who told you that?"

"My instructor."

"And what was this prick's name?"

"Spencer Thrush."

Sandy bursts out laughing.

"You know him?"

"Never heard of him. I imagine that describes most of the planet except his unfortunate students. So, you quit writing? Because of what *Spencer* said? Were you afraid you were going to get better? Wouldn't you love to prove him wrong?"

She has a snappy comeback for that, she's sure, but it doesn't snap out fast enough. The bathroom door opens, Clint emerges in a cloud of steam, and Sandy vanishes, blowing her a kiss. She doesn't blow back. No point. He's gone.

"How was your shower?" Genevieve asks brightly.

***

While Clint goes to hear a few of the papers that interest him—he has a fondness for vampires turns out—Genevieve spends the day in front of the mirror, Sandy behind her gesturing to liven things up, speed them up, slow them down, emote, project. She feels like a musician, and he's the conductor. They work on the voice. She gets into it. She always wanted to act, but like the author thing, it never worked out. Here's her chance.

Sandy tells her she's ready and suggests a dress rehearsal. She gives it everything she's got. When she's done, she hears enthusiastic applause, turns, and it's Clint. She tries not to be disappointed. He's quietly entered the room, is sitting on the edge of the bed. Who knows how long he's been there. Sandy has vanished, as he always does when Clint shows up. *I don't wish to intrude*, he says, but he already has. Way deep. She wanted Sandy's applause for Sandy's words. If she's going to be his phony, she wants to be the best, most authentic phony the world has ever seen. She owes him that at least. The words the world rejected will finally get their chance to shine. They're going to be famous. Or at least that's the plan.

"That was terrific!" Clint exclaims. "I had no idea you could read like that. You nailed the voice."

"Thanks." How would he feel about Sandy's ghost coaching her, coming onto her right under his nose? How will she feel if/when she succumbs?

Clint always seems impressed at her burgeoning abilities, all the new ways she finds to dissemble, like just now: pretending to be a character you've pretended to invent, coached by the dead man whose novel you've stolen, so that you might shine in your debut. Sandy always called his novels "she." Like lots of academics, Clint calls his work, "things." A thing on Puck, a thing on interstitiality, a thing on other peoples' things and how to arrange them into some other thing. A word machine. She pictures the critical wheels grinding, the truth coming down the line, finely tuned and tenured.

Or wouldn't you rather have an epiphany or two or three? First time she heard the term in high school English, Genevieve's Texas translation was "wild hare." For Sandy, they coincided with women. Genevieve is just the latest. That's her epiphany for the day. She's not sure whether it hurts or helps, whether it's her epiphany or the dead man's or both. Do the dead still have epiphanies? They do have erections apparently, and that's perhaps not at all irrelevant in this context. Even if no one could ever possibly read it, part of her, some blazing remnant of her adolescence, would still kill to be a chapter in his life. Theft and deceit seem like minor infractions by comparison. No one will die, no one will see, no one will know but Genevieve. That's the scary part. It's all on her. Sandy's here because of her, her desire, her theft. She often remembers that moment in the attic when the light struck the title page. She wonders how soon she knew she would steal them.

***

There's a cocktail and munchies meet and greet thing where she and Clint are supposed to meet up with Mom. Genevieve experiences wardrobe panic, and they're a little late. Mom—never late to free booze—is already on her merry way, being chatted up by an aging science fiction writer of renown, Pete Hildebrand, narrating the details of his wide-open marriage to her and Serendipity Braithwaite, an eminent scholar of the fantastic who is scheduled to interview Genevieve on Saturday. Pete brightens considerably when the younger, prettier Genevieve enters the circle.

No way, Genevieve thinks, I'd rather fuck a dead man. Fortunately, Clint's at her side. She clutches his arm to indicate how closed their relationship is, with a moat of alligators around it, and Pete focuses his campaign on Ella. "I would've thought you two were sisters!" Hildebrand lies. Mom's into it with this whiskeyish girlish giggle horny old men seem to thrive on. Serendipity doesn't look any too happy about that. She shifts the conversation to the article she's just written about Pete's oeuvre. She actually says "oeuvre." More than once. Pete preens. Ella's impressed with him, her hand on his arm, touching the great one. Serenity's going down. Ella's got this. Genevieve needs a drink. She wonders if Sandy will show up to help navigate these waters, though she's reassured to know, as at any human gathering, she's not the only phony in attendance. Clint wisely wanders off to mingle.

An hour in, she's doing well, finding that if she munches and nods thoughtfully and inquires after their work, most of the scholars are perfectly content to keep talking. She consumes a frightening quantity of mini-quiches and book recommendations. Clint has tucked into a corner with Mirabella somebody, a fantasy writer and scholar whose name in Italian means good-looking, and they sure got that right, like a pre-Raphaelite painting, a look she knows Clint's a sucker for. His eyes keep straying to the woman's russet locks she must spend hours brushing. Looks like Clint would be glad to help her with that. They're intensely talking mythos when Genevieve circles round them. Mythos this, mythos that. Genevieve decides to mythos out on the rest. Saying she must prepare for her reading in a couple of hours, she slips back to the room where Sandy is waiting. He's stretched out on the bed with her laptop in his lap.

"Back so soon?" he says.

"What are you reading?"

"One of your stories Spencer hated —" False Dawn," I think you called it. It's filled with wonderful things."

"The story is stupid."

"You must mean the silly surprise ending. Nothing stupid about it. Just don't make it the ending. Start the story there. Avoid all those contortions you go through to keep the poor cat in the bag. Cats like to come out and play, you know." Sandy hated surprise endings.

She can see it in her mind, her story revised. "What about the title?" Spencer abused it at length. That's how the butchery began—scorn the victim as everyone sharpens their knives

"Don't worry about that. Something better will present itself."

She plucks the laptop from his lap, sets it on the bedside table, and takes its place, pulling his face to hers, kissing his cold mouth. She shakily tries to unbutton his shirt, but her fingers grow numb and stiff in the effort. "I'll do it," he says, and she concentrates on shedding her own clothes.

She pulls him into the bathroom, turns on the shower and pulls him inside when the room is filled with steam. "Fuck me!" she says. "Do it!" After all those years of pretending.

He does. She wants it to be awful, so she'll never do it again. It's not. It's everything she's dreamed repeatedly it would be. Oh darn.

She's still trembling when Clint shows up looking for her. Her reading! It's now, the big event of the evening! She must get dressed! What is she doing naked?! Did she forget?! What's wrong with her?! What was she thinking?! She scurries around the room putting herself together, not bothering to answer Clint's many irrelevant questions. She just made love with her soul mate in the shower. Danae? Wasn't that her name? Perseus's mom. Only difference is Genevieve's birthing his books.

Sandy watches all this with detached amusement. He didn't vanish this time, leisurely putting on his ghost clothes while she and Clint nut out—the living, what can you do? What fools these mortals be. Some help Sandy's turned out to be. Just what she needs before giving her maiden performance as a rising star in the sci-fi, sorry, science fiction, firmament: multiple orgasms. She's a little hoarse. Things got a little vocal. That's okay. It'll work with the character's voice, make her sound tougher than she is.

"Don't forget the book," Sandy reminds her as she's about to leave without it. She scoops it up and clutches it to her chest the whole way.

***

The journey from the hotel room to the podium in front of a banquet hall filled with people is a disjointed blur. Andy introduces her to a dozen people whose names she promptly forgets. Fortunately, everyone's wearing nametags. People take turns saying nice things about her, mostly lies, comparing her work to Woolf's *Orlando* and Swift's *Gulliver's Travels* as well as a string of SF titles she's never heard of. When Sandy wrote it, he likely thought the novel cutting edge, though more than one calls it retro. Doesn't matter. They all love it—smart, fun, a wild ride. She smiles through the praise. These are nice people. They want to like her, and she wants them to. She likes them. That's what matters, isn't it?

Andy wrangles the mike in front of her like strangling a shrieking snake, and there's dead silence, a whisper of feedback. She smiles at the sea of people, the book trembling in her hands, and they smile back. What a dear little prize winner she's turned out to be. She wants to give them what they want, opens the book to chapter one and gives it her all—reading Sandy's words as he's coached her, as if she were a cyber-babe marooned on otherworldly mean streets—another fucking vaga-bond:

A Sandstorm of Destinies

It's like this, as I understand it: Anything can happen in any number of universes at any given moment, and in each moment are nested an infinity of nows. I believe that was the phrase. Don't ask me to explain it. It wasn't *my* job, not my bullshit. This was just pillow talk. Derek trying to be poetic.

Tiny forces exerted in one universe, he said, can produce big results in others if you know what you're doing—or truly fuck things up, if you don't.

I would place myself firmly in the latter category. Unfortunately, I'm the only one here who knows this incalculably unlikely reality we're in was thrown together by an operator who made it after hacking into her roommate's system because she was tripping on shrooms and thought it would be fun.

Bad operator. Very, very bad. That would be me.

I saw Derek type his password. Who uses passwords any-more? He has this system like a trade show from the future. And there he is, typing in a password. I can't help myself. Since I was a kid. I see a password; I use a password. Don't tell me you're not the same. I don't steal anything or black-mail anybody. I just look and leave. Usually.

Derek left, I slipped into his private office—I'd known the door code since forever—and entered the password, played around with the menus in what I thought was a creative fash-ion, though I don't remember it too well now. Eventually, I got bored and hungry and went to the fridge, and all the food was weird. I wondered what was in these shrooms, but I found something that looked like French Fries but green that tasted decent, so I ate those. I went back to Derek's system, but it had timed out and wouldn't take the password.

The operating system was weird too. It didn't seem like the same hardware, so I stopped and looked around. It wasn't Derek's room anymore. Somebody else's stuff was sitting around, pictures of somebody else's folks.

It was Audrey's room. Audrey Strooley, if you can believe. Everything's got her name on it. I made quite a mess ransack-ing the place finding one Strooley thing after another. I ran outside, which is where I am now, outside a building that looks a whole lot like my building if the architect's favorite color had been burnt orange, but it isn't my building, and it confirms this fact by not accepting my code. I can't get back inside.

Welcome to my world—that's not my world. I have no fucking idea how to get out of here. I didn't even know I was here until it was too late.

I try to remember what I did. Derek makes little worldlets for a reason—to see what would happen *if* . . . whatever—it's always a secret. He makes a universe to a client's specs, pinches off a bit of our universe, shapes it, checks it out, files a report, gets paid—a *lot*—which is how he can afford such a nice place. The pinch part in particular, he says, is tricky. I say roommate, but I haven't actually been contributing that much to the rent. He's been letting me hang for a while until I can get my own place. Now I have my own universe.

That's okay in a way. I needed to move on. We started sleeping together. My bad. He's started calling me Cassie. I hate that. When you have a cool name like Cassandra, you like to deploy the whole thing. I tell guys that, but they don't listen. *Cassie, Cass, C.* C.? Seriously? All my shit's inside the apartment. I can't prove who I am. Somehow I don't think the local authorities would accept my Virginia driver's license. I say this because there aren't any cars. Anywhere. Not a single one.

But everything's in English. How unlikely is that? There are lots of people out walking. It takes me a while to figure out what is truly weird. No one is fat. There's a phrase Derek uses all the time. I've never really thought about what it meant: *Proof of concept*. This is a simulation. Only it isn't just a program, it's real. A universe that will go on and on like all universes, with or without me.

I asked him what happened to a universe once he was done with it.

"What do you mean? Nothing happens to it. It just keeps on keeping on."

"Some bullshit universe?"

"Some of them are pretty cool."

"You ever go back, for like a visit?"

"What for?"

"I don't know. The food?" I was hungry. Always am after sex.

He laughed, and that was the end of that discussion.

I couldn't stop thinking about all those abandoned universes. That's how I started when I got into his system, opening up all last year's universes and cutting and pasting and mixing and matching and throwing in something you might not expect—having fun. Tripping. I'm surprised this place seems so normal.

It's a young place. I wonder where the old people are. It's a demographic, I realize, a target audience. So what's the message?

A woman steps in front of me, blocking my path. She has the most pleasant smile on her face. Eerily perfect teeth. We're deep into the uncanny valley. "Cassandra," she says, "I have a message from Derek: 'What in the fuck do you think you're doing, bitch?'"

Cassie's one thing, but *Bitch*? Really? Was that totally necessary? I smile my own sweet smile. "No reply," I say and push past the messenger into the teeming streets ahead. Catch me if you can, asshole.

As I worm my way through the crowd into some sort of bazaar or marketplace, I seem to lose Derek's messenger. I strain to look over the crowd, and I realize I'm taller. I look down at myself, touch to confirm. I'm taller. Also breastless.

With a dick. Still, bi, I assume. I don't have time to ponder because here come what are no doubt cops in any universe from every corner of the plaza.

At a doorway beside a small cafe, a door opens and a woman beckons. A stairway leading up is behind her. Cassandra breaks into a dead run, and the woman disappears up the stairs, and Cassandra follows, closing the door behind her. . .

As the action heats up, Genevieve gets into it—Cassandra's sassy voice, reminiscent of Millicent's in *Don't* whom she spent a good stretch of her adolescence pretending to be, in front of the mirror, walking down the street, scared and expectant, taking ridiculous chances. Cassandra's adventures become her adventures, and she thinks, it's as if Sandy really did write this for me, and only I will know. Our little secret. Huge secret, perhaps. Secrets don't always stay the same size over time. Pretending to be somebody else, she meets herself, and is moved, changed even, buzzing from head to toe with passions both fictional and real for twenty minutes or so, and the two of them—her and Sandy—hold the room spellbound.

There's a long silence, and the place erupts applause, and she cries, not the despairing tears she wept when she learned Sandy was dead, but the incredibly joyful tears that he's come back to life. These stories— she thought she had found them, and they belonged to her now. Truth is, they found her. She belongs to them. Their fates are forever entwined.

Clint and Mirabella, standing shoulder to shoulder, applaud together with equal enthusiasm in the front row. Genevieve wonders if Clint has told her his girlfriend's a fraud, a bad operator, a Judas scholar passing herself off as a real writer. Mom's beside them with some new silver fox on her arm, already past Pete apparently. Roberta gives her a big beaming smile. Genevieve looks over them to the back of the room where Sandy is dancing a jig, his arms raised in two thumbs up. Then he blows her kisses. She can almost feel the chill upon her wet cheeks. She's delighted he liked it, that she's made him so happy. She blows him a kiss back.

The Q & A is mostly process questions, and she goes on at length about her writing practice, stealing it all wholesale from Sandy. After all, that is how this particular novel was written. When it comes to the novel itself, however, she finds she doesn't have to steal, that she trusts herself to speak for the two of them about what the book means and why it was written. She knows him, after all, better than anyone, better than she knows herself.

***

Roberta joins her at the banquet as dessert is being served. Genevieve and Sandy couldn't agree on which dessert, so she's having them all. Sandy steals a taste now and then, and she swats at his hand and hopes no one notices. Chris doesn't. He's on the other side of the table talking *Christabel* and *The Eve of St. Agnes* with Mirabella, having apparently already exhausted *The Ancient Mariner*, the poor old sod. Mirabella's been telling him Russian folktales that have inspired her work and seem to be inspiring him. Roberta says, "We have three offers so far."

Genevieve knows she's been pursuing film options. "For *Sandstorm*?"

"For all of them. With a deal on future properties."

She writes some numbers on a napkin, claiming things could go higher since some haven't made a bid yet, and discreetly shows the napkin to Genevieve who almost chokes on her mousse. She drains her wine. Not just a thief anymore. A rich one. Sandy hasn't said a word. He warned her not to be distracted by the money, which never occurred to her would be a problem until she saw that napkin.

Roberta leaves it for her, a keepsake, as she dashes up to her room for a discussion with the publishing house about promotion. "They want to release you simultaneously, in the four different genres, four different global divisions singing your praises. We might need a bigger napkin."

This one's scary enough for a while. She tucks it away out of sight.

"I loved your reading," the woman next to her says, Marilyn from Ohio who writes mostly short stories. They talk about universes. They talk about the hotel, the con, the field. Marilyn welcomes her. She couldn't feel more grateful or guilt-ridden.

"Should I have told her I'm a fraud?" she asks Sandy.

"Who will that serve? Not me, certainly. Not the novels. The truth will just embarrass a lot of people instead of enjoying your charming company like I am."

You're too sweet, she thinks, just as I imagined you.

***

All is going well in her interview with Serendipity until she asks about Genevieve's science fiction "touchstones," and her mind freezes. She can't think of any major science fiction writers, has read only a few dozen stories. She knows she can't say Mary Shelley. Then she feels Sandy's cold lips at her ear whispering, and mindlessly she repeats him. "Ursula K. Le Guin," she blurts, trying to remember an interview with her somewhere like the *Times* a few years ago. She died not that long ago, Genevieve recalls, but she never paid attention to the obituaries, though they were certainly glowing. She's read nothing, not a word. A murmur of approval runs through the crowd.

"Which Le Guin?" Serendipity inquires—the one of this novel or that novel or this other trilogy or these seminal short stories?—none of which Guinevere knows from Sanskrit poetry. Maybe she should've said Shelley, Huxley, and Orwell and taken the groan, confessed her ignorance.

A member of the audience objects to Serendipity's Le Guin taxonomy and says so, laying out his own with the assumption apparently that Genevieve will settle the matter or join in on the fun. These fantasists are a rowdy bunch. Other voices chime in with amendments and objections. Genevieve opens her mouth, but nothing comes out.

Then Clute rises, all in black, and the mumbling room falls dead silent. He's one of the fellows after whom her prize is named. She met him earlier and found him dear, sweet, and wonderful and really quite brilliant and handsome to boot. He wasn't just smart. Lots of people are smart/too smart and still manage to be a whiny bore. Not him. It was a joy to watch him excitedly tussle with one idea after another as fast as they came to him. He was delightful. He addresses the question in beautifully constructed sentences that take Guinevere's breath away, though she doesn't understand a word of it only partly because she hasn't read a word of Le Guin—though she certainly will, having heard him speak so profoundly of her work. There's a riffle of applause, and Genevieve nods her head as if it's for her—*What he said!*— and they move on to the next question. Disaster averted. She even finds an excuse to talk about *Frankenstein*. Life out of death, a theme with fresh poignancy for her.

***

The rest of the conference for her is mostly a party, hanging out at the poolside bar with throngs of drunken fantasists. Everyone is even nicer drunk. Sandy's always close at hand, but he doesn't butt in. He doesn't want to distract her from her party.

And then at the peak of the festivities, Trevor Hatchette shows up, and Sandy whispers in her ear, "That's him, the guy who slugged me."

"He did? He connected? I could never find confirmation on that."

"Well, you've got it now. The man's a total nutjob."

So, she gathers from the chatter all around her as Hatchette moves through the crowd, being greeted by this one and that one, while others are clearing out of his way hoping to avoid him. The whispers suggest he's been permanently banned from the conference for his past behavior. Yet here he is. He seems to be heading straight for Sandy.

"I thought he couldn't see you," she says to Sandy.

"He can't. It's you he's coming for."

And sure enough, there he is, in her face, in all his glory, Trevor Hatchette, the enfant terrible of SF, Sandy's nemesis, just about everyone else's while he was at it. For such a backwater genre, it had more than its share of bitter internal contentions, but none match the sheer contentiousness of Trevor Hatchette. Boldly go? he often said, over my dead body.

He speaks like a ham actor at a dinner theatre playing a bully. "Isn't it the prize winner? The pretty girl. That explains a lot. A jury of three old men and a couple of dykes pick the hot young thing. How surprising is that? You might not even have had to fuck them. No matter that it's *all* stolen from me. I wrote a novel with the identical premise called *Reality Riots* as an Ace Double before you were born. I furthermore wrote a prize-winning story entitled "Sandstorm" and another called "Destiny." These old fools don't care, but if you think I'm going to let some dumb cunt steal my genius, you have another think coming."

Since he crossed paths with Sandy, she knows who he is and his reputation, how now she's expected to find a lawyer and settle with this douche. Nice work if you can get it. But since she's operating on pure fun kindly provided by the dead through no labor of her own, she says, fuck it. "So you read the novel?"

"I certainly have not. I've been informed of its contents." He waves his phone in the air. Someone had sent him a shot of the ARC jacket copy.

Genevieve cracks up laughing. "You have got to be kidding me. That's all you've got? I say bring it, Trevor, but I gotta say you're looking old, once so hale and hearty. Must be hard for a child to wither. No one even gives a shit about your temper tantrums anymore. I guess you should've been nicer. So fuck you, Trevor. Sue away, you whiny little shit, and take a swing at me if you want, because I know I could kick your sorry shriveled little ass without breaking a sweat."

He must think so too, and he slinks away to his car and roars off into the night, and whatever doubts the science fiction community ever had about her have been banished forever. *You'll never believe what she said to Trever Hatchette!* She'd rather be known as a literary genius, but badass not to be fucked with is second on the list.

Roberta shows up to inform her the publisher wants her to do a Cassandra *series* and the first one isn't even out yet; the one, truth be told, is enigmatic enough to spawn any number of fresh plotlines. Genevieve asks Sandy what she should do.

"Go for it," he says, but then he always says that. Death has not made him less risk averse.

"You'll write them?"

"I'll help."

***

She takes a long hot shower at the end of the night, has been looking forward to it all day. She tries to talk about the Cassandra series, but

Sandy silences her with kisses. No worries. God knows how long they're in there. She'll say one thing for the Marriott, they seem to have an endless fount of steaming hot water. There are a few times she's afraid Clint must hear her primal cries, but by the time she emerges, he's fallen fast asleep and doesn't feel her trembling beside him. It's not entirely from the cold. She thought young men were intense. They're nothing, it seems, compared to the dead. She is bursting with life, scarcely able to sleep, wondering if she can pour this energy into keeping Cassandra alive for a few more books. She ponders Sandy's suggested revision of her old short story as she drifts off to sleep.

**

She and Sandy spend their last day in Florida fucking and talking about his novels and her future career. He pretends not to see a conflict. She's not in the mood to see any either. She's died and gone to Genevieve heaven, though she isn't dead, or doesn't think she is. Maybe this is Genevieve hell. Thing is, she isn't suffering.

Clint does his part by continuing to have long heart-to-hearts with the beautiful and brilliant (he reports) Mirabella. Genevieve wants to feel jealous, but mostly she's glad that Mirabella gives her the chance to see Sandy alone. She's lost track of Mom who got deep into a polyamory discussion over breakfast the first day and seems to be working her way through the discussion group whenever she surfaces.

Beats hearing about BJ.

Sure enough, on the flight back to Richmond she tells Genevieve she'll be heading out to Taos at the end of the week to spend some time with Brian. She says the name like Genevieve should know who that is, so she pretends to, hoping Mom won't tell her. She doesn't whisper a word to Mom about who she's been fucking. *A ghost, Mom. My idol.*

I'm fucking Elvis. So just keep your stuff to yourself. I have enough already.

Chapter Seven

Mystery

The Missing Sister

One would think a writer would be happy here—if a writer is ever happy anywhere.

— Raymond Chandler, The Long Goodbye

Back home things continue the same, she and Sandy together all day getting ready for the next event, all over each other like white on rice as Mom would say. This time Genevieve's a mystery writer, which she's fortunately read a few of, and has a touchstone all ready—Raymond Chandler—ever since Sandy sung his praises in *Thoughts on the Novel* and she devoured everything he wrote in a summer, watched all the tv and movies, none of them quite right, none of them *her* Marlowe. This time she asks Clint if he wants to come along, and he declines. This time they go alone, just her and Sandy, just how she's wanted it to be ever since he appeared to her up at the cabin, how she's wanted it to be pretty much forever.

She's thought about revisiting the crazy hypothesis, that this is all a psycho delusion to assuage her guilt over stealing his manuscripts, but not frequently or for long. Not when haunted is working out so well. Does she really want to talk to a shrink weekly about her screwy mother and her absent father and take drugs when, face it, she doesn't *want* to be cured?

A sparkling young woman named Melody meets them at the airport and takes them to the hotel. She doesn't see Sandy, of course, and talks all the way about men who are dying to meet Genevieve, with a little thumbnail dish on each one. Little do they know that a dead guy has gotten there first. Sandy seems to enjoy all this immensely with an occasional chuckle from the back seat. Melody is halfway through *Missing Persons* and doesn't want to talk about it and ruin anything, but she does have one question: "Were you a twin?"

Genevieve glances at Sandy as if he had some secret twin she doesn't know about, and he shakes his head no. "Research," he says.

"No," Genevieve answers, "but I did a lot of research."

"You so nailed it. I have these twin cousins? . . ."

The rest of the way they're regaled with twin stories.

"Is this how you did your research?" Genevieve whispers to Sandy when they reach the hotel. She remembers him saying, "Most of the important research for a novel is best done in a bar or a bus station or the middle of nowhere."

"Mostly," he confesses. "I had twin sisters-in-law for some years. Laura and Kathy. I hung out with them quite a bit. Later on, they quit speaking when one of them married an asshole the other couldn't abide. They were sort of the spark for the book. They had this powerful connection they loved and despised. I tried to imagine."

That was when he was married to the shrill one who called him Wilkie. Genevieve had missed the twin information somehow. She wondered what other gaps there were in her knowledge of him. So, she's not crazy: Sandy's ghost just told her something about himself she hadn't known before. Crazy can't do that, can it? She remembers talk of the sisters-in-law in correspondence, little more than their names, but always together—Laura and Kathy—like twins. By her calculation, they must be at least in their mid-sixties by now. She wonders what became of them.

She and Sandy wander around the convention hotel, an old burgundy carpet and curlicues sort of place from the teens and twenties, upgraded to modern quality with a bit of the ambient spookiness remaining. The perfect location for a gathering of pretend detectives.

Mystery's all about the past, Sandy says—setting it right so the present can get back on course. I thought it was about murder, she says. That's best, he agrees. Nothing mires us in the past more than a dead body washing ashore, a life unaccounted for, but a long-lost friend showing up or taking off will do just as well. Read Chandler, he suggests: He's the man. But she already knows that. How did she get onto Chandler in the first place? By reading what Sandy said about him, of course. He'd never steered her wrong, except for dismissing SF.

In one of the darker stretches of the somber hallways, a woman steps up beside Genevieve and says, "I'm Chloe. Has my brother bothered to tell you about me?'

Her brother, Genevieve assumes, is the absent Clint. The resemblance is unmistakable. "You're Clint's sister. You ran away at fifteen." He said she was beautiful and intense when she left. That part hasn't changed. Though intense might've slipped right on into spooky. She does some quick math in her head. Mid-thirties now. Thirty-four or thirty-five. Evidently homeless no more, she looks like just another svelte jogger in pricey togs setting out for a run.

Chloe makes a face: *Such lies!* "Not true. *Told* to leave. Thrown out of the house. An important distinction omitted in the official record of my departure. She knows it too, Mom—the Great Detective. She's the one who told me to go, that she'd lost all patience, not that she ever had much. 'Get the fuck out and don't ever come back' were her exact

99

words. Then when she had second thoughts, she went to detective school and had herself declared the patron saint of poor unfortunate missing children. You ever catch her on TV advising desperate parents with that fucking pig Dr. Phil? Don't let her fool you. She's just atoning for her sins."

Genevieve wonders what any of this has to do with her. "And what's the plan, are you just going to keep that pissed-at-Mom meter running? What's it been? Going on twenty years?"

"She threw me out."

"I got that part. You look like you're doing okay, probably have your own place now, I'm guessing. So, what do you want with me? I hardly know the woman. We had the new-girlfriend-with-Mom brunch. You were a footnote in the tragic tale. I *never* watch Dr. Phil, by the way, and I'm not about to start now. Now here you are. I have my own bad mom to deal with. Join the club. Your brother misses you, by the way. So he says, anyway. No reason to lie to me."

She laughs. "Everyone's lying to you."

"Like who?"

"Like little brother. The name Mirabella ring any bells?"

Loud and clear, like an anvil chorus. "Why do you ask?"

"Because it was wall-to-wall Mirabella last time we spoke. That's what he's doing while you're here, hooking up with her for a romantic weekend in Asheville. I exist outside of time for him, beyond the reach of cause and effect—the rebellious runaway forever. It never occurs to him I might have an opinion about the life he leads. I wouldn't worry overly about Mirabella. Mom will make short work of her. She always does."

"I thought he hasn't heard from you since he was a kid, had no idea where you were."

"The last part is true. I keep it that way, but he's sworn to secrecy, and like Mom always says, 'Clint is true.'" She chomps her teeth together like a dog on a bone and laughs. "Mom's so full of shit."

"So why are you ratting him out?"

Chloe shrugs. "I thought you should know what you're getting into. Little brother loves to fall in love and does so at every opportunity." She looks around trying to decide whether to tell her the next part, the part she's come here to tell Genevieve obviously: "Little brother ratted you out, told me all the details of the thing you're doing with the dead guy's books. Thought it was hilarious and couldn't wait to tell Mom. I told him he was being a dick. They're a predatory team those two, been doing this for years. Clint falls and Mom pounces. Run for the exits."

Slack-jawed, Genevieve doesn't know what to ask first.

Chloe's eyes go wide, and she jerks her head back, looking past Genevieve's shoulder. "Clint!" she cries and Genevieve turns, but there's no one there, turns again and Chloe's gone.

"Did you see that?" Genevieve asks Sandy who's been hovering in the gloom the whole time. "She just ran off."

"Indeed. It was positively thrilling." He's gazing after where the lithe Chloe must've dashed.

She glares at him. "It was, or she was?"

"Can't it be both? You'll have to admit she has a flare for the dramatic—a certain willowy intensity."

"And beauty."

"There's that. You can see the resemblance to your young scholar gypsy—though not so bland as he."

"What the hell does she want with me? She tracked me down here, knew Clint wasn't going to be here. Why tell me her sad story?"

"So you will *tell* it, of course. That's what you are now, you know, a storyteller. Might as well get used to it. I can't count the lives narrated to me in transit or at parties once people heard what I did for a living. People want their stories told for all sorts of reasons. For starters, Chloe wants to sing the same old blues: Mom's a fucking phony and a disappointment to the planet and has smothered/crushed/destroyed my once limitless potential. Sounds like she's pissed at Mom and Little Brother both. I wouldn't get in the middle of that—a mama's boy and a mama lion."

"What about that business about their being a predatory team?"

"We'll just have to see if she pounces as promised. Meanwhile, what are you going to do about Clint and Amazonia?"

She laughs. "Mirabella."

"Her as well."

"Do you have some wise council? Some more of that dead wisdom of yours."

"Let him go. He's a waste of time."

"Just like that."

"Just like that."

"That's the best you got? How do I know you're not lying to keep me for yourself?"

"You don't. Sounds quite romantic when I hear you say it, like one of my heroes, daffy with love. Not that I'm not, but that's not it. He's not up to you, Genevieve, pure and simple. It's obvious."

"And you are?"

"No, I'm dead, so all that nonsense is behind me. I don't have to keep up. You are always before me. I am who I am and will never betray you. The choice is easy."

"Truth or lies?"

"No, life or death. Besides, he ratted you out to his sister, and I'll never tell a soul, at least not a living one."

Melody approaches from down the hall and calls to her, "There you are! There are some people in the bar who are dying to meet you!"

And then Sandy's gone, leaving her to ponder, she supposes. Choose truth! Choose life! Still, one may lead a life of lies, and death may be the only truth. And what if a dead man is the one who makes you feel truly alive?

She started to object that she doesn't even know for sure that what Chloe told her was even true, but she knows. Clint's fucking Amazonia, all right. In Asheville, no less. In some romantic little inn he'd never dream of taking Genevieve. That should max his credit cards. Good for him. Clint is doing what he wants to do. As am I, she admits to herself. As am I. So why do I keep pretending I'm not?

"I can't wait," she says to Melody following her to the dark, oaken bar filled with literary sleuths at happy hour.

"They have little sausages and $2 shots," Melody confides excitedly.

***

"Have you seen this?" Roberta asks, plopping down beside Genevieve at breakfast, flashing her tablet at her.

The mystery guys, mostly guys, like doing shots in the hotel bar, makes them feel like a detective in one of their books. It was a late night. Genevieve plans to spend the morning guzzling coffee, seeing nothing but the buffet. She has panels and things all afternoon. She hopes not to fall asleep. One of them is on interesting and original ways to kill your characters. She should be in the right frame of mind for that, feeling half dead herself.

"I've seen nothing." She reluctantly accepts the proffered tablet. Confirming her suspicion that he haunts Roberta to keep up with their joint career, Sandy shows up for this. She can feel his frosty breath as he reads over her shoulder. It's *The Washington Post*. The headline reads, "Now That She's Written Everything, What Will She Write Next?" There's her surrounded by the future covers of her four "prize-winning" novels. She hasn't even seen them yet. The ARCs were rushed into print before the covers were done. They're trying for a similar look in four different genres. She's a brand already. The article's hook is the four "first novels" that won or placed in four different genres, to be published simultaneously with massive promotion, including a push to start Genevieve Book Clubs throughout the known universe. She wishes they said more about the work and less about the business and the "unheard of phenomenon" they go on and on about. "They call her The Everything Girl," says the article, not making it clear who "they" is. Girl? Really? She sighs. What is she complaining about? If it was telling the truth it should read The Nothing Woman.

"Not bad for a dead guy," Sandy says, and Genevieve laughs.

"Pretty incredible, huh?" Roberta looks dazed. "I've been on the phone ever since this came out. My voicemail's full. You ready to do some interviews?"

"Who with?"

"Who do you want?" She rattles them off. Pretty much everybody. In a quick consult with Sandy, they settle on all the NPR and PBS programs, *The Daily Show*, and *60 Minutes*.

"Don't forget the list," Sandy reminds her. Shortly after they checked in, sprawled in their suite in post-coital bliss, Sandy suggested some addenda to her publishing and film contracts, the details of which were still being hammered out. He insisted she write them down and give them to Roberta. She almost forgot. She slides the list across the table and digs into her huevos rancheros with sour cream as Roberta reads. A waffle waits in the wings.

Roberta keeps glancing up, shaking her head, arching her eyebrows. The list makes an impression. Finally, she says, "I thought you didn't know anything about the industry."

"I'm a quick study."

"I'd say so. Yesterday at this time, I would've said as a new writer you would never get half this stuff, especially this degree of control. Today? Sure. I'll give it a try. How's Monday for Morning Edition?"

"Day after tomorrow?"

"Yes."

"Say yes, Genevieve," Sandy whispers, and she does. It's on him to get her ready, the master of the NPR interview.

"I saved the best for last," Roberta reveals. This is the real mind blower: "Jennifer Lawrence wants to meet you. They approached her about playing Cassandra in the series, and she wasn't interested, *but* she was interested in you—playing you in a movie, telling your incredible story. The Everything Girl." Incredible. Not to be believed. Just the word for it.

Sandy roars with laughter, obviously imagining what Genevieve's imagining—the real story on the screen—though he may be enjoying the Jennifer Lawrence part on a whole other level. Genevieve's laughing too. She can't stop. She manages to sputter out, "My *story*? *Crime doesn't pay!*" which Roberta takes to be some weak joke about writing crime fiction.

***

Genevieve hoped to enjoy being runner-up better than winner—all the perks but none of the pressure, but the word soon spreads like wildfire that a newly hatched celebrity is in their midst soon to be on *60 Minutes*, scheduled for an audience with Jennifer Lawrence, a streaming science fiction series in the midst of a bidding war between HBO, Netflix, and Amazon, staggering advances for her four "first novels." The list goes on. The winner of the prize, poor guy, can't get a toast at the bar, while she trails mystery writers like bloodhounds wherever she goes.

She's on a panel about influences, and since some of Sandy's books can be seen as mysteries of a sort, she sings his praises as a major influence—"on all her work." And of course, once she starts talking about the work of Gene Sanders Wilkerson, there's no stopping her. Her mother used to tell her to get a life, and she had, in books, eight novels in particular. No wonder she feels so alive since she's ingested five new ones all at once. It's like they're growing inside her. She even draws comparisons between her work and his—How Lyle in *Missing Persons* is a mirror image of Rick in *Without Regret*, only it would have to be a funhouse mirror since Lyle is long and lean, and Rick is short and stocky. She gets a laugh, even though few of them have likely read *Regret*. Some of them are ordering it from Amazon before the session's over. She imagines his sales rank climbing and smiles. Maybe some real good can come out of this after all.

Sandy watches from the sidelines. The room is packed with people who want to see The Everything Girl. He appears delighted by her performance. Is that because he likes what I'm saying, she wonders, or because I'm owning the lie? As every good novelist should, Sandy says, but he was talking about fiction, not life, though Genevieve's long disregarded the distinction.

***

She likes the mystery writers. They're mostly a bunch of nerds, like any gathering of writers, like most of the guys she's dated, but they all have these tough guy on the mean streets author photos in the program that make her smile. There are plenty of women. Same story. Tough broad on the mean streets. Most of them live in some bland suburb like Genevieve grew up in before Dad split. What meanness there was, beside the usual family horror show, was all inside the houses. In books filled with murder and mayhem on the bedside table.

She talks author photos with them her last night there. Roberta's scheduled a shoot week after next when her round of conferences is over. They all agree that four different author photos for the four different genres only makes sense: Cyber Chick, Sexy Sleuth, Hot Paramour, Brooding Intellectual (in glasses). She'll have to get a new pair.

"No dogs!" one shouts his advice from the end of the bar.

Once again, they've all had quite a bit to drink.

Genevieve looks at Sandy who tilts his head and arches a brow— it's up to her. "*All* dogs!" she decides and gets a round of applause, because at this point, they will side with her on anything, and they order another round.

Sandy witnesses this more somberly. She knows what he's thinking: You never know when the wheel of fortune will turn again, and you'll be trapped in the attic with nothing more to steal, while angry villagers threaten to burn the place down. Enjoy it while you can.

She imagines going to the SPCA when they get back to Richmond to get a dog and wonders briefly what Clint would think of the idea but realizes it doesn't matter. She and Clint are over. There's no turning back now. Besides, the dog will have to wait until after all this travel.

***

When she returns home, she's resolved to sit down with Clint and sort things out. Like laundry. They're down to that. Whatever they had going dissolved once Sandy showed up. She isn't looking forward to explaining herself without revealing the true cause of her transformation, which Clint must imagine is just the simple act of thievery and deceit she's already confessed, her sudden good fortune. She can't claim Sandy's love and approval, his passion—his complicity. She can't decide *what* to say.

Turns out she doesn't have to say anything. Instead of Clint, it's Tanya at the kitchen table having avocado toast, her bag still sitting on the sofa. "He's not home," she says. "How was your conference?"

Let's see if she pounces as promised. The woman doesn't waste any time. "Interesting. Fun. You here long?"

"Just passing through. Business. I saw the story about you in *The Post*. That's what you're running from, isn't it, dear? That crazy implausible story? 'Four First Novels!' The Everything Girl!'"

"But nonetheless true," Genevieve says, testing Tanya's reputed lie detecting abilities and Clint's discretion. Chloe said he was dying to tell Mom, not that he did.

Tanya laughs darkly. She knows. Genevieve chose the wrong confessor. Happens often as not in a Wilkerson novel. She should've seen it coming. Clint can't lie to Mom, might as well tell her everything.

Sandy walks through the backdoor and takes the stool beside Tanya, eyes her avocado toast, smiles rakishly at Genevieve.

"I saw Chloe," Genevieve tells Roberta, hoping to rattle her.

"I know. I followed her there."

Jeez. And Genevieve thought her family was fucked up. Genevieve feels like bait. What do they want with me? she wonders. What'd I do? "You're too fucking much, the two of you. *Find* her already and be done with it. And when you do, say you're sorry even if you didn't do anything wrong. *Or* fucking leave her alone. Find less ironic employment. I don't want any part of it. So, where's Clint? Did you say?"

"You don't know?"

"Only what Chloe told me, that he's in Asheville screwing Mirabella. She didn't give me an address or a duration. I thought he would be back by now. He has classes tomorrow."

"He told me what you did. He's only now realizing the gravity of the situation, the possible legal jeopardy your reckless behavior has placed him in."

Sandy and Genevieve roll their eyes. Of course Clint told her. That's the kind of boy Clint is. He tells Mom everything. She's the one who ladles on the gravity. He's true, all right, just not to Genevieve. "Whatever do you mean?" She doesn't even try to sound convincing.

"I believe you know."

"Is this what brings you back to Richmond? Your little boy's exgirlfriend's supposed evil deeds?"

"I had an interview to conduct."

"Let me guess. Grandma lied to you about Little Pumpkin."

"How did you know?"

"How did you not? Everybody lies about their Little Pumpkin. I do." She cuts Sandy a meaningful glance. *I'm not telling* anyone *about you.*

Sandy makes a face, obviously displeased to be described as her Little Pumpkin. But there it was: He is. He sneaks a bite of Tanya's avocado toast more for Genevieve's amusement than anything else. Play. That's what Sandy's all about. That's what she loves about him. Sandy used to say that the best writing is always play. She's never had a Little Pumpkin before, somebody she'd lie for—because to tell the truth would be to lose them.

Tanya gobbles down the last of her toast. "Clint asked me to remind you that this is his apartment, and he expects you to be moved out before he returns on Wednesday."

"With Mirabella."

"Yes. It will be better this way. For all concerned."

From all appearances, Mirabella's made for him, if he's made for anyone. Or maybe she's just the next one if what Chloe says is true. Either way, it's not her concern.

Genevieve doesn't debate the point. She just packs and leaves. Fortunately, she still has her place since the lease runs through the school year, and most of her stuff, her books in particular, are still there. Most particularly, her first editions of Sandy's books.

Sandy leaves her alone as she makes the long drive back home, so she can cry her tears for Clint in privacy. There are surprisingly few. Some for the love lost, more for the betrayal, plus a few choice words.

Sandy shows up at dusk. Since he's never been here, she shows him around, meaning they do a 360 in the middle of the room—books, books, books, bed, bathroom, books, kitchen, card table. "I love it," he says. "Just as I pictured it."

"You imagined my digs?"

"Of course. Didn't you imagine living in my home when you were there? You spent the night several times, as I recall."

"You were there for that?"

"Indeed."

"Then you must've seen me lying in the meadow masturbating in the moonlight."

"I did."

"Do you want to know what I was imagining?"

"Of course."

"This moment." She pulls him into her narrow bed, and they melt into one another until all the chill is gone.

***

They throw together a dinner and eat sitting up in bed. "What do you think Tanya's going to do with her newfound information?" Genevieve asks him.

"Oh, rat you out, I would imagine. Some time when she might share the spotlight, add a bit of polish to her brilliant detective career. Exposing a fraud is even better than rescuing runaways."

"She can't prove anything."

He doesn't say anything, but she can hear in his silence the opinion that no one needs to prove anything to derail the Everything Girl train. All it will take is the whiff of a hoax, and she'll go from feel-good phenomenon to yet another fucking fraud.

Or maybe Tanya won't do anything. Maybe Clint will stop his mother from exposing Genevieve for the sake of his feelings for her. Maybe not. Probably not. Not. Tanya's coming after her.

All she can do is keep on keeping on with her busy schedule. She does *Morning Edition* tomorrow, flies to Ft. Worth Tuesday for the romance convention, then on to Literature in Tucson right after. She won't have time to bother moving out her stuff before her Wednesday deadline. There's not that much anyway. No worries. She'll buy new. She can afford it now. Clint and Amazonia will just have to deal with the remnants of her presence.

She has too much else to worry about, more audiences to deceive and delight. Clint will be much happier with Amazonia.

As for herself, Genevieve watches Sandy as he browses through her books—mostly Wilkerson favorites—totally absorbed, perusing her scribbled marginalia with a loving smile on his face and can't imagine ever being happier than here and now. Let tomorrow come. She's ready.

***

She does the *Morning Edition* interview, and she hardly has to say anything, so excited is the breathless interviewer to share all the good news of her spectacular, unprecedented success! The interviewer keeps circling back to Jennifer Lawrence like a bee to clover, clearly wishing that Jennifer would play *her* in a movie.

She has Genevieve read the opening of *Missing Persons*, even though she was going to read from *Willingly*—which she's rehearsed—but somebody decided it was too hot for the morning commute and said, "Do the mystery instead."

So, totally cold, she's got to jump into a noir sad sack with a yearning for his lost love on half a cup of coffee. She isn't prepared for how it makes her feel, identifying with Lyle, who like Tanya is in the business of finding missing persons, and like Tanya, there's a story behind it. In Lyle's case—in Genevieve's—the search is for the love of their life, though in Lyle's case you don't know if she's alive or dead, while Genevieve may not have flesh and blood, she's got certainty and obsession. They give her ten minutes, a radio eternity, and she's afraid she's awful, though Sandy reassures her along the way she's doing splendidly. It's weird reading to no one but the person beside you and millions of people you can't see—just her and Lyle and the whole wide world where his love might be anywhere. She pores herself into him.

Missing Persons

It was a game the four of us played from time to time: if you were shipwrecked, alone on a desert island, what would you want with you?

What book?

What tool?

What game?

What movie?

Only things. People were against the rules, because you weren't alone anymore. The closest we came to people was pets, but since Carol's allergic to damn near everything but fish, it didn't go anywhere.

We'd say our thing and talk about it. Argue about it. Confess our little secrets. We thought, in this way, we were getting to know each other. It was like one of those philosophy classes I took too many of in college: We were four unheard trees falling in the forest, describing how we'd sound if, and only if, there were no one else to hear our unique, but predictable, thuds. We didn't have a professor to point out that what we thought we wanted, and what we actually would want if we were, in fact, all alone, weren't necessarily the same thing. Doesn't matter. Playing the game, what we wanted was to create a character for the other three, the person we wished to reveal to the others. The stories made up of the stuff we chose and why we chose it. Looking for missing persons, I usually only have what they left behind to work with. If I had an inventory of what they took with them, I could find them in no time. Our game was fun. It was risky. I say the other three, but for me it was always about Elise.

The night we did movies, Carol objected because there'd be no power on the island. She strove to uphold realism on her island, while the rest of us had grown weary of realism and were willing to throw a solar-powered entertainment center into the doomed ship's consignment to get the question on the table.

It was David's turn to go first, and he said *The Seventh Seal*.

Elise burst out laughing, shook her head and muttered, "David, you're so full of shit," as he explained over her infectious laughter what an uplifting experience it would be at the end of another long, hard day on a desert island fighting for your survival and your sanity to watch *The Seventh Seal*.

"My film professor in college said it was the greatest film ever made," David said.

Elise rolled her large brown eyes, slowly, like someone taking in a long breath. "He was a *graduate* student, David, and let him watch it on his desert island. We're asking you about yours. It'd serve you right to be stuck with the goddamn *Seventh Seal* for day after day."

Elise knew him too well to believe him. They'd been married for three years. "How many times have you seen it, David?" she asked him, then turned to us, the jury.

David pretended to think hard, adding up all those times. Finally, he said "Two."

As usual, I threw in my lot with Elise. "Two? That's it?"

"It's an intense experience."

Carol said, "Maybe David means it would be different on a desert island, that somehow that experience would call for *The Seventh Seal*."

I knew for a fact she hated any movies in black and white or with subtitles and had probably never seen *The Seventh*

Seal but was only siding with David because I had sided with Elise.

Carol is my wife. Was my wife, I should say. At the time, when I knew Elise. And David.

Elise pointed at the shelves of videotapes and DVDs on the wall. David never threw anything away; he just built more shelves. "He doesn't even own a copy. He has every movie Jamie Lee Curtis ever made, but no *Seventh Seal*."

"Do you really have every movie Jamie Lee Curtis ever made?" I asked David.

He gave an embarrassed grin. "I confess."

"Can I borrow them some time?" I asked, and everybody laughed.

It was another night, when we'd gone camping together, passing a joint around a campfire, that our game betrayed me. I was the third or fourth one. I hadn't been paying that much attention. I was supposed to say whose photograph of some-one of the opposite sex—other than my spouse's—I'd have with me on that desert island. It seemed safe enough before I said it. I later heard from Carol that the others had all named attractive or inspiring celebrities. Carol herself had said Albert Einstein, but like I said, I hadn't been listening, I'd been watch-ing: The way Elise's chin rested on her slender hand, the way the firelight played across the contours of her face, the way her eyes registered each emotion. I looked across the camp-fire at her and spoke without thinking. "Elise," I said, and they were all too embarrassed to speak. No one could manage to make a joke of it. Especially me. Everyone knew, I suppose, that I was besotted with her, but no one was supposed to say so.

After a while, a pair of owls started calling back and forth to each other across the hollow. The fire had died down to coals, the cold seeping into our clothes, but no one put another log on the fire. The wood was cut and stacked, two paces off.

Finally, I couldn't stand it anymore, so I stood up and stirred the coals, tossed a few sticks on the fire. The owls had moved on up the hollow. Their hoots echoed down to us, blurring and merging into a single, faint cadence. The sticks smoked and caught.

Carol said, "Does anybody know what kind of owls those are?"

And I said, "Great horned owls." We were all too literate not to make something symbolic of that—cuckolds, demons, harpies—but nobody said anything. The faintest smile played at the corners of Elise's mouth in the firelight.

***

We all went on as if nothing had happened, though we never played the desert island game again. The next year, David and Elise moved to Dallas. The year after that, Carol moved to Seattle. Without me. I hadn't spoken to Elise or David in over ten years, until last week when he called me up. She was missing. He wanted me to find her.

They were divorced now too, had been for some time. "But we were supposed to meet for dinner," he said. "We were working on getting back together, or at least I hoped we were. When she stood me up, I was just hurt, but when she didn't show for work, I got really worried." He took a deep, shaky breath. It rattled against the phone. I could hear cars in the background. A semi roared by. He was calling from his car parked on the side of the road it sounded like. "I heard from Carol you have a business finding people."

There was a long silence on the other end of the line, filled with more trucks roaring by, then a faint chorus of crickets. Where was he? Who was he looking for?

I didn't even know Carol knew about my change in profession from IT drone to private detective. We didn't stay in touch except her Christmas cards every year to everyone she knew, even me, with a little gossipy note in each one. That's probably where David had heard about my change of profession. What little I knew about David and Elise, I had from Carol's cards. Not surprisingly, she hadn't mentioned their divorce to me. "How long has she been gone?"

"Two weeks."

"You called the police?"

"Of course."

"What do they say?"

"That apparently she left of her own free will, and there's nothing they can do."

"Why do they say that?"

He sighed again. "She closed out her checking account the day before, stopped her mail, no forwarding address. Her car's gone. The house is locked up, though it looks like everything's inside. A kid at a gas station near her house remembers her filling her car up at four o'clock in the morning, had him check the oil, told him she was going on a long trip, but she didn't say where."

It was the next question, but I always hated to ask it: "Was she alone?"

It took a long while for him to answer. At first I didn't think he'd heard the question. Finally, he said, "She had a guy with her. The kid at the gas station said they were pretty friendly."

I felt sorry for him. To have Elise and lose her. Twice. I couldn't imagine. So, without thinking much whether I had any business looking for Elise, I agreed to check some things out. "I can find most people without ever leaving my house," I assured him. "I could use some information to work with. Can you get into her place?"

He hesitated. "I guess so."

"My advice still stands. If you're afraid of what you're going to find out, let it lie."

"No. I can get into her house. What do you need?"

I told him exactly what to look for: bank statements, credit card bills, insurance policies, personal correspondence, emails, texts. See what she left behind she might be coming back for. Most important, a list of what she seems to have taken with her. He wrote it all down, the crickets chirping away in the background, said he'd send it to me right away. I got a long email a couple of hours after I hung up the phone. He had it all—even a photo of her birth certificate. I blew it up and ran my fingers over the tiny whorls of her footprints and went looking online, confident I'd find her in an hour or two.

***

After searching for a couple of weeks, I knew I wasn't going to find her the easy way. She hadn't used any of her credit cards since the day she left, hadn't gotten a traffic ticket or been arrested anywhere in North America, hadn't purchased a plane or train ticket, hadn't sold or purchased a car, and wasn't employed. She could be anywhere, and her trail was a month old, practically frozen. After that long, most things are forgotten by all but a handful of people—if they're remembered at all. I'm never surprised when people forget the face of someone I know for a fact bought gas from them two days before. It's when they remember, when two months later they can tell you about the dent in one of the hubcaps, the way a perfume smelled. Something was going on then. It always meant something.

Me, I could remember the day I met Elise better than I remember my father's funeral, better than I remember my first date with Carol. I didn't have to catch the scent; I'd never lost it. I wanted to find her, had always wanted to, even when she was right there in front of me, and I was married to someone else and so was she. Now, looks like, we're both single.

I called David up and told him what I'd found—nothing. "David, I hate to say this, but I have to agree with the cops on this one. She got a wild hare and took off. Let it go."

But of course, he didn't let it go, wouldn't. By the time most people call me, they've got the scent, they've got to go after some idea in their heads about what this missing person

119

means. It's gone way beyond the object of their search. It's the search itself that keeps them going. Sometimes they're actually disappointed when I find their missing person, even if the reunion is a happy one. Because the search is over, and now they have nothing to hope for anymore.

I had the feeling that David wasn't going to find the Elise he was looking for, but I figured if I didn't help him, he'd find someone else who would. I shuddered at some of the possibilities, guys who'd show him movies, *Found your wife. Nice fleshtones on the guy's ass don't you think?*

So, I flew to Dallas and met David at his office, trying to convince myself I was just helping out an old friend. I didn't succeed. I was on a quest to find Elise on that desert island, at long last, just the two of us.

Chapter Eight

Romance

The Novel Thief's Daughter

Who were you thinking of
When we were making love
Last night?

—*The Texas Tornados*

She's read science fiction and mysteries and some hot romances, faking her way through three genres—she figures being ABD at twenty-five checks the Literature box big time—but how in the world do you prepare yourself for Jennifer Fucking Lawrence? Who wants to *play* you in the story of your fucking made-up life? Not to mention *60 Minutes! 60 Minutes?* Seriously? She poses these questions and many more to Sandy, not really expecting any answers. She likes that he gets that. Most men don't in her experience. They want to fix her like she's a broken radio or a flat tire.

They're walking hand-in-hand in downtown Ft. Worth where the romance convention—a huge thing, 8000 or more—is being held. The other two were puny by comparison. She checked in and slipped out of the hotel to walk around before jumping into the fray. She's been unloading on Sandy practically the whole time, while he admires the classic skyscrapers and listens patiently. When Vivian in *Don't* is on the run, she passes through DFW but never makes it into town. Neither has Sandy. This is Genevieve's stomping ground.

She's scheduled for scads of promotion and marketing panels. No surprise. The *60 Minutes* crew is showing up some time today. Everyone wants to know the secret of her success—interviewers, instant fans, hungry writers—but she can't reveal it: That she's a thieving little ghost fucker, which she, herself, has come to terms with, but can't exactly share with the curious public. It's all completely wonderful except for the niggling little fact that she didn't write a word of her impressive oeuvre except for a smattering of edits and revisions and most of the hotter sex in *Willingly*.

"You'll figure it out," Sandy says during a lull in her rambling lament, meaning the fame, the spotlight.

"Easy for you to say," she says, though she knows better from his correspondence. Being an overnight sensation was a day at the beach with tsunami. If he hadn't drunkenly agreed to help crew a boat with a madman, broken his leg, and written *Death By Beauty* out of sheer boredom, the world would have no idea who he was.

"Only because I have such faith in you. I figured it out, more or less, and you're a lot more together than I ever was."

She eyes him critically, but he seems to be sincere. "Thanks. Were you always this sweet when you were alive?" Then why all those divorces? Could her soul mate theory be true?

"Definitely not. Death instructs, resets one's priorities. Gives you too much perspective to believe your own bullshit. Nobody ever wanted to do a biopic about me, however. You should definitely insist on writing the screenplay for that yourself, by the way."

"I don't know how to write a screenplay."

"You're forgetting—you're The Everything Girl. What *will* she write next? Who better to write her own story? How hard can it be? Whatever you decide you want that story to be—the movie will matter way more than your real life. Cut yourself out of the loop and they can say any damn thing they please. Better your damn things than theirs, wouldn't you say?"

"I say, how about forget the whole thing. A movie about me? The novel thief?"

"How about *The Novel Thief's Daughter*?" They'd had a hilariously good time in Barnes & Noble last week finding all the offspring titles—daughters, sons, bastards. Daughters definitely led the pack.

He makes her laugh again, his sole intent. "Fuck you, Sandy."

"Is that what you'll say to Jennifer Lawrence?"

"No lies! That's what I'd like to say. Hold nothing back."

"Even me?"

"*Especially* you. You've made the whole thing happen. You wrote every word. Who do you think should play you?"

"I'll leave that up to you and Jennifer. Someone devilishly hand-some, I assume."

"You know I'm only kidding, right?"

"So, what is your intention? To invent a better truth—something noble and inspiring for those who hope to ascend to your literary heights?"

Ouch. "I take it back about you being sweet."

"You'll ascend, you'll see. Stop worrying so much. Enjoy yourself. Write the screenplay. I've always wanted to do one. Never got around to it. Saw enough of my work butchered at others' hands to last several lifetimes. Come on, my darling. We can collaborate. It'll be fun."

Though all of his novels were optioned, some repeatedly, only one made it into production, an embarrassingly awful version of *Don't*. Genevieve's read all the screenplays. There are dozens, all truly awful. None by Sandy himself. "What the hell. I'll tell Roberta in the morn-ing."

"When do we meet Jennifer Lawrence?" he asks.

She swats him in mock jealousy. "Attempt to be cool. They're still working it out. Soonish."

"Soonish."

"That's what I was told. Roberta said I might not have much warning. They're trying to work me into her busy schedule. She could just show up. I'd rather not think about it. We have a romance convention to wow. Roberta says the *60 Minutes* crew will be here following me around. Do you think it would be okay if I wear a bag over my head?"

Sandy holds her close and rocks her in his arms. "Don't worry. Everything will be wonderful." He doesn't seem so cold anymore, more like a pleasant chill. She doesn't know whether that's because he's warmed or she's grown used to him. Naturally, it's plenty warm in Ft. Worth.

It's been awhile since she's been back to Texas, and she spots what she's looking for, what she's missed most about the place—a small Mexican diner where she can gorge. "Do you like Tex-Mex?" she asks Sandy.

"*Por supuesto, mi querida,*" he replies.

"Follow me."

They sit in a corner booth, and Genevieve orders enough food for three people. It comes right away, and they dig in. "Try this, try this, try this," she says, and she can't tell what he's saying, his mouth full of food, but she knows the sounds of pleasure when she hears them. When they hit grazing pace, she gets coffee and a praline and tries to prepare herself for another literary world.

"So, what's romance about?" she asks him, "if SF is about change and mystery is about the past, what is romance about?"

"Yearning. And sex, of course. Intense on both counts. Though generally there's more yearning than sex."

"Yearning's pretty much nonstop, isn't it?"

"Even unto death in my experience."

"And then?"

"Then there's no more life to lead—to lead you where you long to go. Everything stops. No flesh and blood. Only, now that I find I have a life again, yearning—and romance—have returned refreshed many times over from their long slumber, rather like Sleeping Beauty."

She likes that many times over part. Even though many times zero is zero. "A . . . a life?"

"With you."

Is that a lump in her throat? Definitely. Tears brimming. She says, "You want to go up to the room?"

She downs her coffee and saves the rest of the praline for later, leaves the food on the table. Only for love would she walk away from an untouched chile relleno.

***

From the romances she's read, purloined from her mom's bedside table, she agrees with Sandy's assessment. Yearning and sex, something she knows a little about. So, she'd hoped to be talking about sex and seduction, powerful longing and happily ever after. Escape and momentary satisfaction for passionate fans. More yearning, more sex. She totally gets the genre's attraction, though for the moment she's feeling fairly satisfied.

But the overwhelming majority of the attendees, nearly all women, seem to be aspiring writers. Their yearning is intense all right, but they lust after careers in books clad in jackets featuring muscled Adonises—the cover models for which, roaming about like mountain gorillas posing for selfies—are a draw as blatant as bikini babes in a Bud Lite commercial. There's a refreshing honesty about the romance world she finds immensely appealing, despite the ingrained snobbery of her English major indoctrination where romance was held in even lower regard than science fiction, if that were possible. Except for St. Jane Austen, of course, and the Brontë pantheon.

She gives a "workshop," consisting mostly of her ad libbing her way through the "Scene" chapter in Sandy's *Thoughts on the Novel.* She reads them the "Perfect Stranger" quote, and they love it, love her. She doesn't tell them they're really loving Sandy, though she drops his name several times, and their phones are busy boosting his Amazon sales.

On a panel about balancing your life and your career, she confesses to not having much of a life before, and now that she has this instant overwhelming career, she's open to any suggestions on how to deal, and that gets laughter and applause. Everyone beams as *60 Minutes* cameras pan the crowd. Once again everybody's nice, offering ideas for not totally losing her mind while not blaming her in the least if she does. And maybe they all hate her guts in their heart of envious hearts, but she doesn't think so. Sisterhood is powerful. *If she can do it, I can do it*, they're thinking, and that's what they want to think, and she wants it for them too. Not the thievery part, but the success, whatever it takes for them to feel like a Real Writer. That's why they're here, and Genevieve would be the last person in the world to fault them for that. She's spent most of her life wanting to be a real writer, and though you can certainly quibble about just what that means, stealing from a dead man doesn't exactly put you inside the tent.

If they knew her real story, would they hate her then or merely pity her?

Sandy's right. She needs to lighten up, but when you seemingly have everything you've ever wanted but it's all a charade, it's hard not to think about much else, especially when others admire the pretense and wish they were you. But real. Where's the happily-ever-after in that?

When the *60 Minutes* crew takes a break for an early dinner before shooting the evening's events, Genevieve sits down at the bar alone and orders a margarita. It's five o'clock somewhere, as Mom always says, though usually midmorning. Genevieve watches the muted television as just so many shifting shapes, zones out, and sips. Her passion-chapped lips burn from the salt. She's only vaguely aware of someone sitting down beside her.

"Genevieve," a voice says. "Long time."

She turns. Not that long. Four years. Prentice, her first poet. Anemically handsome. Intense. Jerk. He's the one who read a venomous villanelle about her at his thesis reading that got way too much applause. "Prentice," she says. "How's it going in Oklahoma?"

"Arkansas. State college in the Ozarks. It's nice, peaceful, a lovely setting. I have a lot of time to write. I hear you've been quite the prolific one, winning prizes and everything."

Sandy sidles up and sits on the other side of Prentice, leans around him to inquire, "Who's this asshole?"

"Don't worry about it," she says.

"I'm not," Prentice replies, thinking she was speaking to him. "I just wonder who actually wrote them. It couldn't possibly be you. Remember—I've read your dreadful fiction, dear. Tell me—where *did* they come from?" He tries to come across as an eager confidante instead of a rooting rodent, but doesn't come close to pulling it off. Same dick as he ever was.

"The depths of my tortured soul, *dear*. Just like when you excrete your poetry."

He takes the insult with the expression of a man who knows her to be a philistine whose barbaric opinion is beneath his contempt. "Someone came by my office to discuss you. Imagine my surprise. A private investigator. Wanted to know if I was familiar with your work since her sources told her we were once intimate."

"Intimate. Is that what we were?"

He tries to look hurt. "I told her you couldn't possibly have written a decent novel, much less four of them, that your short stories were rather like bad *Twilight Zone* episodes."

"Five."

"Pardon?"

"I wrote *five* novels. Four won prizes and are getting all the attention. Did this investigator say why she was so curious?"

"She said fraud is suspected. That the novels were almost certainly stolen."

"Stolen? How does one steal a novel?"

"She didn't say. I was hoping you might shed some light."

"Is that what brings you to Texas? I didn't figure you as a romance fan."

He shudders with revulsion. "Hardly. I'm visiting my sister in Arlington. I saw your picture in *The Star-Telegram*. Couldn't pass up the opportunity to see you again. The genre *pays* well, I understand."

If you want to piss off a poet and make them mean, tell them you get paid for your work. Even though they're all ravenous for grants and prizes, they pretend to prefer the purity of poverty, then lament they're underpaid and underappreciated, the unacknowledged legislators of the world. "Well enough. Though I'm being paid rather more than most, not counting the movie options, of course. You tenured yet at this little mountain shithole where you teach? Let me guess. You're poetry editor for some little rag you publish your pals in so they'll return the favor."

Sandy is enjoying this. He gives her a thumbs up and a wink. *Give it to him, my darling!*

Prentice hops down from his perch and draws himself up. "They're going to nail your ass, Genevieve, and I'm going to love every minute of it." He stalks out of the bar in a hammy huff. Poets. They don't need a movie. They're in their own biopic 24/7.

"What did you do to him?" Sandy asks.

"Two things. I'm smarter, and I didn't fake orgasms. I thought his poetry sucked, but I would never say that, but then I didn't gush either."

"Trying out dialogue?" a big bear of a man says from beside her. He's white haired and a little shaggy, but very sweet and pleasant, like an aged chocolate Labradoodle.

"Yes," Genevieve manages. The Everything Girl talks to herself.

"Sounds like an interesting story. I'm Bobby Boisseau." He offers his hand.

"I'm Genevieve Slidell." She shakes.

"Oh, I know who you are. Can't believe I found you alone. I heard you were from Texas and wanted to meet you. Liked your book. Reminds me of something I'd write when I was writing as Nicole Le Noir but a few degrees hotter." He fans himself with fluttering hands. "I'm always too timid."

Genevieve laughs. "Glad you liked it. The editor wanted me to crank it up. You write under a different name now?"

"Use my own. My husband and I are a team, write historical series. Still love stories—nothing like a love story—but with the Alamo or outlaws or something Texas thrown in. Dell, my husband, loves that stuff, does all the research. We do okay with them."

The bartender delivers his white wine, and Bobby offers to buy her another margarita so they can sit down and tell lies to each other—they're both Texans, after all—and she gladly accepts.

He asks if the rumors are true that the Cassandra SF book is going to be a series—books and TV—and she says, "I've heard the same rumors. Certainly didn't plan it that way." She tells him she's thinking about a screenplay.

"That's what Dell wants to do—adapt our novels into movies and make some serious money—but I'm getting too old for all that bother. You're young and eager. If you decide to write more romances, it's not a bad row to hoe. You can do damn near anything you want these days as long as there's love and hope. Supernatural, mystery, sci-fi. S & M—whatever—there's a romance flavor for it. Romance readers are up for damn near anything as long as you bring the love and fellows like him." He nods toward the bar where a muscled cover model is downing a glass of ice water between events.

"I'd love to meet Dell," she says. "Is he here?"

"Oh, he hates these things. You here with someone?"

For a few seconds she almost tells him the truth, that just the other side of him, taking in their conversation with wry amusement sits the love of her life, trusting that Nicole Le Noir would understand that we're not all who we seem to be, but of course, she can't. "On my own," she says. "Just me and *60 Minutes*."

He laughs big. "You going to the karaoke this evening?"

"I wouldn't miss it even if *60 Minutes* hadn't insisted. They seem to think me making an even bigger fool of myself will endear me to their viewers."

Hours later she and Bobby do a rowdy duet of "Who Were You Thinkin' Of" by the Texas Tornados, bring down the house, and leave the *60 Minutes* crew beaming.

Sandy too. He adores her. She's always wanted to be adored but has never felt adorable, quite the opposite. Too good to be true? But isn't that what romance is all about? What Genevieve wishes she could confess to her warm and welcoming romance friends is that she never wrote a romance, but because of one, she's in her own, willingly. No regrets. Guilt and terror, but no regrets.

***

Waiting for their plane, she checks her email, stuffed with fan letters, many of which call her an inspiration, and several have manuscripts attached for her consideration, hoping some of her magic will rub off on them. She remembers some of the names from the conferences, recalls their starry-eyed hopefulness. How can she say no? How can she find time to read them all?

Sandy offers to read them.

"Seriously?"

"I always believed in giving back. My own success was such a fluke."

"Not as flukey as mine. What will you tell them if they're awful?"

"That they show promise and should continue to revise—can't hurt one way or the other. No one should write unless they love doing it, long past the first draft. They'll either give it up or get better. Their choice, not mine."

She's been revising her short story following his suggestions and getting into it but isn't quite ready to show it to him yet. She's been equally surprised by how truly awful it was and how much better it's becoming with revision. She hopes he wasn't just leading her on. He once compared revision to reincarnation. Keep at it and even a slug can eventually achieve nirvana.

This reminds her of something she's been pondering in the back of her mind—why her favorite of the purloined novels was shunned by the judges. She jotted down a few pages of notes, and they've been riding around in her jeans pocket next to her phone. "I was thinking about revising *The Mad Statue*. A lot has happened since you wrote it, and I thought I might be able to update it, so to speak."

He seems taken aback by the suggestion, even though he tries to hide it. So, it's okay to critique my work, she thinks, but not the other way around? "I . . . I suppose that would be all right. What . . . what did you have in mind?"

His doubt that she's up to the task is a little too obvious. "Never mind," she says and turns her attention back to her inbox. Tellingly, he doesn't pursue the matter as she struggles with her hurt feelings.

She almost overlooks the deadly missive from *feslidell*.

Franklin Earnest Slidell, D.D.S.

Subject Line: Bravo!

Dear Gennie,

I've been delighted to read about your great success! You were always such an imaginative little girl! It just so happens I will be in Tucson for a Dentist's convention at the same time you are scheduled to be honored! I am so proud! I would love to see you! It's been much too long!

Love,
Daddy

Daddy? *Love,* Daddy? Seriously? Much too long? Seventeen fucking years! She rereads it several times. Every exclamation point is a like a dagger through her heart. She starts sobbing and almost misses her plane. It's only by virtue of Sandy's gentle guidance that she finds her First Class seat and secures a glass of champagne. And then another.

The pilot points out the Grand Canyon below, and Genevieve sees it as just an enormous ditch, the Slough of Despond.

She tells Sandy she wants to face Literature on her own.

"Are you sure?" he asks. "They're rather meaner than the other genres. They have to maintain their borders, you know, keep out the riff-raff." Sandy was always a marginal citizen in the world of Literature until after his death—too popular by half. Apparently he still nurses the wounds.

"I want you to stay away. I have to handle this one on my own. You don't think I can do it?"

He's much too wise to touch that. She doesn't think she can handle it, why should he? But he would never, ever say so.

When they touch down on the tarmac, she glances over, and the seat's empty. She's alone, her perfect stranger gone. She couldn't stand to confess the truth even to him, the real reason she ran him off—Sandy and Daddy in the same place would be way too much to handle.

Seventeen years, nothing. Then Love Daddy. That fame's some powerful juju. She's not too crazy about its latest trick. Not too crazy yet. Let's just see how crazy she can get.

Chapter Nine

Literature

Down at the End of Lonely Street

In this idea originated the plan of the 'Lyrical Ballads'; in which it was agreed, that my endeavours should be directed to persons and characters supernatural, or at least romantic, yet so as to transfer from our inward nature a human interest and a semblance of truth sufficient to procure for these shadows of imagination that willing suspension of disbelief for the moment, which constitutes poetic faith.
—Samuel Taylor Coleridge, Biographia Literaria

It's fucking huge. 12,000 writers, teachers, students, editors, booksellers, agents, et al, all here for Literature. It's totally overwhelming even without *60 Minutes* dogging her footsteps through the cavernous convention complex, all the while on the furtive lookout for Daddy. He might turn up anywhere. Will she know him? Will she care? By the time she has her badge, schedule, and book bag, she's a frazzled mess.

The vibe here is definitely not good, like *Why is 60 Minutes on the trail of that bitch instead of someone who writes Real Literature—a Real Writer?* Everyone asks her where she teaches, where she got her MFA. "Nowhere" doesn't seem to be an acceptable answer to either question. She could confess to ABD, but she's already kicked that one to the curb. She told her dissertation director, employer, most powerful motherfucker in the department to go fuck himself in a myriad of ways. *Dr.* Slidell ain't happening unless she decides to become a chiropractor.

Those who have heard her story aren't thrilled to have a multi-genre sensation in their midst. When they use the word "genre" you'd think it was a synonym for "trash," or worse, "popular." *Multi*-genre? Slut. There's a buzz in the air. She can feel it. The tide is turning. It might be desert outside, but there's a tsunami on its way. Why the fuck did I tell Sandy to sit this one out? she asks herself repeatedly. Daddy. Because of Daddy, always Daddy. So, where the fuck is Daddy?

She retreats to her room and pours over the pages of *Scapegoat Phoenix* she's scheduled to read in the morning as if it's a noose to be tied. She practices reading the opening as she imagines Sandy might want it read, but her tongue dries up in her mouth, and she feels as if she's wandering through the desert herself. Himself. Because the narrator of *Scapegoat* is a man, a boy, Isaac, son of Abraham, who talks to the Daddy in the sky, all set in Phoenix, a couple hours away on the Interstate through pretty much nothing. Stupendously beautiful nothing. God tells Abraham to kill his son and sacrifice him. Abraham has the boy tote the firewood. It isn't clear whether God had a say in that sadistic decision or not. The Bible story enraged Sandy. He wrote about it on several occasions. It broke Genevieve's heart. She totally understands the character. She works at being him. It's hard because she can't stand to look at herself in the mirror. The Everything Girl going down in flames.

She throws the book on the floor and digs through the book bag looking for the schedule, when, sure enough, she finds another copy of *Scapegoat* covered with glowing blurbs. All the glowing blurbage in the world won't help her if Tanya spills the beans and tells the world what her little boy told her about Lying Slidell.

136

She looks over the rest of her schedule and it gets worse: Mirabella, turns out, is here to accept accolades for her short story, "The Winnowing Winds," published in *The Purple Cow Quarterly*, and Clint is sure to be here to applaud her. Genevieve's on a panel with her called "Maintaining Literary Standards"—presumably because they're both prize winners—moderated by none other than Spencer Thrush, her loathsome nemesis who persuaded her once and for all that she couldn't and never would write for shit. According to the program, he's now a full professor at Crenshaw-Atticus College, though it doesn't bother to say where the hell that is. The one bright spot is that she's on a panel about the work of Gene Sanders Wilkerson called "Wilkerson and the Canon," somewhat dimmed by the fact that she'll be sharing the stage with Dr. Bent Morely, former boss and douche bag and leading scholar in the field.

She can't imagine how matters could get any worse until she's descending the escalator to the opening cocktail mix and mingle event where the prize winners, she's been warned, will be introduced and toasted, when she spots Tanya in the crowd beside Clint and Mirabella with none other than Tom Wilkerson in tow, scowling at the assemblage of literati, flanked by aged twins who must be Laura and Kathy. Prentice lurks to one side, and then, as if in slow motion, the *60 Minutes* crew wheels about to encircle the group, talk show celebrity Tanya in the middle, a boom mike hovering above her like a cherub awaiting the annunciation. Genevieve doesn't wait to see if Tanya destroys her but wheels about and charges up the down escalator shoving people out of her way and dashing to her room.

The shit's hit the fan. Never was the expression so apt, Genevieve muses, as she slides the chain lock into place.

Flaubert thought the writer should be, like God, invisible in his work. Ungodly Genevieve can do that. She was invisible her entire adolescence. She credits Daddy. The only thing she still has that was from him is an old manual typewriter with an X that doesn't work. So, Genevieve learned to write her first stories without any X's, though sometimes she had to go back and insert them by hand. The X's got fancier and fancier until she wrote a story with as many X's as she could possibly manage—"Flexible Felix's Anxious Exploits." She showed it to her dad who had to appear interested since he'd given her the damn typewriter. "The X is broken," he said, as if somehow after making all those lovingly rendered X's on the paper in his hands, she might not know this. He didn't even try to read the story, a stirring tale of her cat Felix braving a tornado like the one that had terrified Genevieve the week before. Daddy just handed it back with a smile. "Nice." A week later Felix was run over by a car.

A month after Daddy left, she wrote him a long letter on that type-writer—no X's—having convinced herself that that's why he gave it to her, so that they could keep in touch while he was out in the world finding himself with the hygienist, but he never answered. Too soon? Too late? Who knew?

It's been too long. You think? Fuck you, Daddy. You have no idea. She makes a mental list of all the therapists she should call—*You know the absent father I rattled on and on about? Get a load of the email he just sent me after seventeen years!* There aren't enough billable hours in the world to fix this one.

The logo for the fucking conference features a typewriter. Seriously? Who in this fucking building stuffed with writers of all stripes uses a fucking typewriter? Are they the only real writers, then? The typewriter ribbon on her X-less machine was worn to a frazzle, so she found another still in its cellophane wrapper at a thrift shop, though the spools were different, so she had to strip the ribbon off the new one and wind it around the old to make it work. When Mom saw her hands, she said, "What the hell you been into, Child? Your fingers are as black as tar!" Genevieve glances at them now. Her sins are invisible; it's virtue that stains. She would've done anything for that typewriter, but nothing was ever going to bring that X back. It's on the top shelf of her closet, the closest thing she's got to an attic. Maybe it's time to move it to the trashcan in the alley.

Her phone pings repeatedly as she paces the room with increasingly desperate messages from *60 Minutes*, the event organizers, Roberta . . . Even the room phone starts going off. She should really answer it. There's not just this intro/toast thing. Anderson Cooper's supposed to fly in tonight to start their interview, though last she heard, his flight was delayed. The plan is for him to snare her at the party after she's been toasted—the symbolic pinnacle of her literary tour, the embrace of the Literary establishment—and they'll take it from there. They gave her possible questions, but she can't look. She wants to appear genuine and spontaneous and not the sneaky little weasel she is.

There's a light tapping on the door, and for a glorious moment she thinks it might be Sandy come to rescue her, but that doesn't make any sense. If it were Sandy, he'd simply walk through the door without knocking. Except she told him to stay away, and he's respecting her wishes. Her stupid, ill-conceived wishes. For a dead white guy, he's surprisingly sensitive to her needs. She peers out the peephole, and it's Chloe casting furtive glances up and down the hall as if she fears being seen. What a nutjob. The whole family. Why did she think Clint was perfectly normal? Why did she think she wanted perfectly normal in the first place? That's how you end up with the truly weird. She opens the door, and Chloe rushes inside.

"Mom's downstairs talking to the press. I wanted to warn you."

"Is she going to rat me out?"

"I doubt it. Not yet. This is just the tease. She'll wait until the hype amps up, let the press check out the entourage and speculate what she's got up her sleeve, get the backstory out there, before she starts making the rounds of the talk shows. This is all about building name recognition for the brand. She'll sacrifice your fame to fuel her own."

"Makes sense. I'm Isaac. I brought my own firewood."

Chloe cocks her head in confusion and gives her a quizzical look.

"Bible stuff," Genevieve explains, and Chloe shrugs her indifference to the subject. Lucky girl. "I was about to get hammered. My very next step was that little old mini fridge over there just bulging with booze. Want to join me?"

Genevieve doesn't wait for an answer. There's a split of champagne in the mini fridge. Genevieve pops it open, pours two plastic cups full, takes a big bubbly gulp and hands the other to Chloe. "That's why Tom's here, I take it, as the wronged party, the victim of my Machiavellian machinations."

Chloe laughs. "Sounds like you might be a couple drinks ahead of me."

"I had some champagne and a couple of shots of rum on the plane." She was trying to prepare for meeting Jennifer Lawrence by watching old interviews. One night, Colbert kept giving her shots of rum and Jennifer made it look totally fun getting wasted on national television, and Genevieve wanted to be her, or even better, the other way around.

"Tom?" Chloe tries to remember, holding out her glass for a refill. "You talking about the old guy? He says his big brother wrote them all."

That empties Genevieve's glass. She pops another split, and the cork rocks the ugly lamp by the bedside table. "How the hell would Tom know? He never gave a shit about anything Sandy wrote his whole life. Now that Sandy's dead, he's just trying to cash in."

Chloe doesn't ask whether Tom's claim is true. She's already chosen sides: Not Mom's.

"How do you know all this?" Genevieve asks. "Surely Tanya didn't tell you."

"Whatshisname, Prentice. I've been watching them since they got here this morning. They all had a big lunch, then he went for a swim. I pretended to be a sore loser in a bikini, and he told me everything while he put sunscreen on my back. He must really hate you. What are you going to do?"

"Sit here and drink this champagne until it's all gone, then take it from there." That's what a Wilkerson heroine would do—wing it. She wishes she had some pot, wonders if Chloe might have some but doesn't ask. When she wants to be totally irresponsible, pot works way better than alcohol.

There's another knock at the door, and they both jump and Chloe giggles. Should've asked about the pot. Genevieve tiptoes to the door—totally unnecessary on the carpeted floor, but wildly hysterical to Chloe, and peeks out. "It's Clint," she says, not sure whether she's surprised or mortified, and Chloe's laughter becomes a strangled bark like a dog hitting the end of its chain.

"I don't want him to find me here!" Chloe pleads, and Genevieve points to the closet.

Once Chloe's inside the closet, Genevieve opens the door wide and invites Clint in with a sweep of her arm. "Come in, I 'm just having some celebratory champagne, like a wedding guest or an Asheville tourist. Thanks for the knife in the back, by the way. The best part was hearing it from Mommy Dearest."

He winces at her Mom baiting—tough on a mama's boy—but rises above it. "I'm sorry. I truly am."

"That's all you've got?"

"I knew you didn't love me. I was just a convenient layover."

"Unbelievable. You didn't love *me*."

"True, but I wanted to. Seemed right after you told me everything. Why in the world did you do that?"

"*That's* why you ratted me out to your sister and mother? Your mother, the *detective*?"

"What was I supposed to do? I hardly knew you—and here it is this huge charade. Why would you trust anyone with that information? You couldn't untell it, I couldn't unlisten. When you started winning all those prizes, I had to tell *someone*."

"Not someone. You had to tell Mom. I really thought you were in love with me."

"Really? You didn't seem to."

She shrugs. No use arguing that insignificant point. He never did. It's clear now. Given how little she cares, she didn't love him either. This clearly isn't their story.

"So why the fuck are you here?"

"I'm trying to help you, if you'll give me the chance. Mom's willing to give you the chance to confess it was a stunt that you planned from the beginning to bring Wilkerson's undiscovered work the credit it deserves, and it was never your intention to accept credit for them—which is why you confided in me and Mom beforehand as someone the public would trust."

Genevieve can't help but admire the craftsmanship of the lie. She could make that shit work, sell it, just so long as Tom and Tanya weren't on her tail, but at her side making the tour from Ellen to Anderson and beyond. Maybe even Oprah. Maybe there's a ram in the thicket after all.

"What do they get?'

"Tom gets all rights to the five novels, and Tanya will represent you in the process of returning the literary children to their true home, for which Tom is paying her a percentage."

The literary children bit is too much. Besides, Sandy would rather throw all five manuscripts down Tom's outhouse than have him making a dime off them. "Jeez, Clint! Who the fuck came up with that one? My Literary Children, fuck you very much, are staying right where they are. You can tell Mom, as we say in Texas, she can stick it where the sun don't shine."

Chloe bursts out of the closet applauding. Clint doesn't look any too glad to see her. "What the fuck are you doing here, Clint? This is all about Mom, isn't it? This was all her idea. You're sick, you know that? *When* did you tell her? I bet it was the night Genevieve told you."

Genevieve would tell them that everything about them was about Mom, but figures they already know. She can also see in the pathetic droop of Clint's shoulders that Chloe's accusation about the timing of his betrayal is dead on.

Genevieve is marshaling her righteousness for a withering attack on her deceitful ex-lover, but then there's another knock at the door.

She looks out the peephole and there's Mom and BJ, making out. Considering the alternatives, Genevieve's almost glad to see them. She opens the door and welcomes them in, makes introductions, opens wide the mini fridge to BJ's delight.

"You got any bourbon in there, Sweetheart?" he drawls.

"Sure thing." She hands BJ two tiny bottles of Black Jack. "Mom?" She eyes the empty splits. "Any more champagne, darlin'?"

"No, but I got some rosé."

"Then bring it on."

"What about you, Clint?"

"I— I'll have a beer, I guess. An IPA if you have it."

Like she wouldn't know that. How soon we forget.

She selects some Beefeater's for herself, opens the jar of plump stuffed olives. She pours the gin over a half dozen. They look like a pod of tiny round manatees hiding on the bottom from motorboats. BJ might have pot. Maybe she doesn't need it. She tastes the salty cold gin, and it reminds her of Sandy. She opens a box of goldfish and passes it around.

Chloe has some of Mom's rosé. BJ proposes a toast to Genevieve the prize winner, and plastic cups wobble skyward. "To Literature," Genevieve amends and drinks right down to the manatees, then devours their gin-soaked bodies one by one.

BJ has Clint and Chloe trapped in the corner when they'd probably prefer to be fighting, giving them a discourse on the ins and outs, ups and downs of drywall. Genevieve says to Mom, "You took him back."

"What can you do?"

"Have fun in Taos with Bruce?"

"Bryan. It was okay. Nice house. Pretty views."

"Shitty sex?"

"'fraid so. I'm so proud of you, darlin'."

If Tanya's let the cat out of the bag, Mom and BJ don't know it yet. Clint keeps checking his phone, trying to slip away. Having told Ella the cockamamie story in the first place, he doesn't want to be the one to burst her bubble, apparently. Besides, Mama Tanya must be waiting impatiently for her answer. Just as Genevieve thinks this, there's another knock at the door.

She's positively prescient. Who does she see through the peephole in the slightly rounded hallway this time? Tom and Tanya, of course. They're not making out. That would be too weird. Genevieve throws open the door, and there they are, and just off, out of peephole range lurks Mirabella, of course. Everyone's wondering what's become of Clint apparently, the boy on a mission for his mommy.

"Come in! Come in! We're just having a few drinks. Name your poison. Nothing for you, Tom? That's right. You don't drink. Tanya? Nothing? Mirabella? How's Perrier? Looks like Clint could use another brew." She hands her both and sends her off to the drywall panel where she latches onto Clint's arm. *Mine*, she seems to say. No worries, sister.

Tanya says to her boy, "Did you tell her my offer?"

He nods soberly. Tanya finds this inexplicable given Genevieve's giddy mood. Perhaps the bitch is hysterical? "And what did she say?"

Clint hesitates to quote her, so Genevieve delivers the line loud and clear: "She said you can stick it where the sun don't shine!" She devours the last besotted manatee and belches.

"You'll regret this, my dear."

"Bite me, my dear."

Ella steps toward Tanya, fists balled, to defend her only daughter against she knows not what, but then there's another knock at the door, and everyone freezes and doesn't make a sound except for Genevieve who laughs out loud and opens the door without even looking.

It's Roberta! Great! She gives her a big drunken hug. Roberta's brought her own drink in a real glass from the cocktail party down below. "What's going on? They're freaking out down there. Two of their prize winners MIA. Do I want to know who all these people are?"

Genevieve introduces her all around, saving Tanya for last. Tanya declares as she shakes Roberta's hand, "Do you realize that your client is a complete fraud, that the five novels you represent were all in fact written by this man's deceased brother, the famed novelist, Gene Sanders Wilkerson? She admitted this to my son, Clint, a professor of

Literature." She says it like Clint's a priest or a district attorney or a regular on CSI.

"Four," Roberta says. "I only represent four novels. I passed on the fifth. Is this true, Genevieve?"

Genevieve freezes, all eyes on her, and then, inexplicably, the fortune she's carried around in her wallet for the past several months flits through her brain. It's worn to a frazzle, but she's read its message scores of times now, waiting for this moment: *When crossroads flood, another way must be found.* She hasn't studied literature her whole life for nothing. If the X is busted, make it part of the story. True? False? We're talking fiction here. Things are a lot more nuanced than that. "Of course not. My so-called confession to Clint was a story idea for a screenplay I've been working on that I was trying out on him as a sort of metafictional joke." You can park a 747 in the metafictional hangar. Five of them. She sells it with a knowing metafictional laugh.

Roberta smiles. Belief? Disbelief? It's a lot more nuanced than that. But willing suspension of disbelief is easier when you're weighing 15% of millions against 15% of nada. She laughs. Not a that's-total-bullshit laugh, but a how-delightful laugh. In metafictional world they're next door neighbors. Perfect.

She and Genevieve face their accuser as a united front. Ella and BJ have no idea what's going on. Tanya, Mirabella, and Clint leave in a huff. Chloe, Ella, and BJ all opt to see what's going on downstairs where the *hors d'oeuvres* smell amazing and soon follow.

That leaves Genevieve and Roberta. Roberta says, "I always wondered: How did you do it? Hoard these books and not do anything with them, then all of a sudden believe in them all at once? I get self-doubt. I hear that all the time. But how did you find faith in them all? Did you find Jesus or something else equally weird?"

"Something like that." Met their maker. *Turns out he was mine too.*

"I'll go downstairs and get you out of whatever's going on tonight. Then I'll make myself scarce so the press can't ask me what I know. You have my cell. Text me if you need anything. They'll still sue, you know. The old guy looks like he's counting the money already."

"I'm counting on it. Jury trial," Genevieve says. "Courtroom drama. Add another genre to the mix." She makes another drink with the last Beefeater's and another pod of olives. There's an outline of the screenplay on her laptop and in the cloud. Sandy's promised to help. Roberta looks pleased and sets out on her mission.

***

Finally, Genevieve's alone. She knows what to do, what she's been wanting to do since she hit the room. She falls to her knees beside the bed and assumes the prayerful position: "Sandy! Sandy! Sandy! Please come! I was *so* wrong! I can't do this without you! You warned me, but I wouldn't listen! Come get your fucking award before I kill them all!"

She opens her eyes and Lydia is sprawled on the bed, as she must've looked in Sandy's mind's eye when she posed for Dante in *Willingly*.

"You poor thing," she says. "You truly adore him, don't you?" She says this sweetly, sympathetically even.

"Yeah, but I guess you know that already. We haven't been that subtle."

"Don't worry. I haven't paid that much attention. The dead know less than you might think—and more."

"More?"

"They know death. Sandy can't let go of his fortunate life. Who can blame him? He wants to share it with you, the next chapter. Go for it. Why not? He adores you."

147

"Until he adores someone else."

"No one else can see him."

"I have your blessing?"

"That's a little too creepy. I just want him to be happy."

"But what about the mess I'm in?"

"I like the metafictional story. I'd stick with that. See what Sandy thinks." Her eyes go to the closed door, and Genevieve looks over her shoulder.

Sandy walks through the door and Genevieve flees Lydia and throws her arms around him, smothering him with kisses. "I'm so, so glad to see you," she says over and over. "I love you so much!"

He finally manages to ask, after a passionate roll in the hay wherein Lydia had most recently lain, "What does Sandy think about what?"

So, she tells him everything, of course—the rest of the story—and he loves it.

***

They're both asleep when an hour or so later there's another furtive rap on the door. She doesn't hear it at first, and he wakes her. "Someone's there," he whispers, pointing, and she goes to see.

"My God! It's Jennifer Lawrence!" She's disguised in a floppy hat and frumpy clothes, but there's no mistaking who it is.

"You have to let her in!" Sandy whispers, though there's no need for him to whisper. No one else can hear him but Genevieve.

She opens the door.

Jennifer Lawrence enters talking, tosses the hat on a chair. "I can't believe what I just heard downstairs. The Everything Girl is a total fraud! A nefarious villain! Imagine my disappointment after coming all this way to meet you, only to find you're just another ordinary person unworthy of the big screen and a star of my stature!"

Genevieve is mortified and hangs her head in shame. "I'm so terribly sorry!"

Jennifer bursts out laughing. "Just kidding!"

"You don't hate me?"

"Are you kidding me? This is *so* much more interesting! Roberta says you want to write it. What do you have in mind?" Jennifer's eyes scan the abandoned bottles and plastic cups.

"Rum?" Genevieve asks, and Jennifer grins.

Genevieve explains how she was just kidding with Clint, trying out the idea for a screenplay where she finds the five novels written by some old white guy, like everything is. How she came up with the story out of her own sense of Unworthiness to be a Real Writer, so much does she love Literature, but it doesn't love her back. The five novels are all the same story—the longing to get your story told. The treatment's almost done. Just the trial and the HEA—happily ever after—left to go. Jennifer especially likes the part where Sandy's ghost is her accomplice and inspiration and lover.

They discuss the trial, because there will be a trial, metafictional or not. Genevieve lays out her strategy. Jennifer's delighted by the cast of characters, the twists and turns of the argument, the ups and downs of the heroine's—Jennifer's—fortunes.

"Do I get to cross-examine?" she asks with a wicked grin and a husky laugh.

"Fuck yeah! Why not?"

When the rum is gone, they strike a handshake deal, leaving even Sandy starry-eyed and speechless. "I'll be in touch," Jennifer says and is gone as abruptly as she arrived.

***

Genevieve awakens to a massive hangover and the message that she's been cancelled from the awards ceremony and her panels, pending an investigation of the matter. *60 Minutes* says Anderson Cooper will be indefinitely delayed.

Somehow they forget to cancel her from the prizewinners' reading, so she shows up for that, pages in hand, precipitating a minor panic. They expected her to be hiding under a rock somewhere. She smiles serenely, and they give her five minutes at the end. She steps up to the podium in a packed auditorium, more filing in all the time. Word has spread quickly that the cheeky fraud plans to read anyway, and no one wants to miss her disgraceful performance.

No one introduces her. She wrestles the mike into place and just starts reading in the voice of a weary dead man walking:

Scapegoat Phoenix

He dragged me out of bed from a sound sleep for a dawn trek into the desert. He had me toting a bundle of firewood, while he had a coil of rope and a gas can, his machete hanging from his belt.

"What the fuck, Dad," I said.

"Shut up," he said.

We walked into the rising sun, the sand shimmering, lizards idly watching us as we passed. The wood was heavy, blood trickled from a splinter in my thumb, but I didn't say anything. My dad's a crazy fuck. Clear nights, he stands in the yard and talks to the sky, a billion stars blazing, all talking to him, telling him to do things, Mom and me cowering inside.

Every once in a while, he'd sweep his arm to encompass our fifteen acre desert ranch—if it's still a ranch when all the live-stock's dead—and claim, "This will all be yours!" when all I ever really wanted was to get away, the only thing keeping me was Mom clinging to my arm. He didn't tell her what she got out of his deal with the heavens. She already knew. A world of shit, and me. His seed.

We came to a low hill and trudged up a switchback to the summit. Halfway up a coiled rattler reared its head, and the sound of its rattle was deafening, but Dad didn't slow down. He pulled out his machete and lopped its head off. "Get thee behind me, Satan," he muttered. Dad said that often—at the television, in the drive-thru at McDonald's, at the students sunbathing on the University lawn. The rattler kept rattling even as its head tumbled down the hill, and I scuttled past, the load of wood digging into my arms. I didn't know how much longer I could keep my grip.

He pointed to a fire ring on the summit filled with bleached out beer cans. "There."

The sun blazed just above the ridge line. I could feel the heat in my face. It was going to be a scorcher. I dropped the wood on the cans. He waved with the back of his hand like I should already know what to do without being told, forgetting the gods don't say shit to me. "Build a fire. Don't light it yet."

"What for?" He cut me a look, and I thought he might smack me. "So I know what kind of fire to build. What's it for?"

"A sacrifice."

I recalled the bull last spring when the heavens told Dad to lop off the bull's head with his machete, but as sharp as the fucking thing is, he didn't exactly manage the job in one blow and chased the bull around the yard hacking away at it for what seemed like hours until it finally fell to the earth and bled out, Dad shouting "Hallelujah! Praise the Lord!" Coyotes came in the night and dragged the carcass away, so we never even had a taste of the ritual flesh.

I didn't know what the hell we had to sacrifice unless he was hallucinating goats now too. I made it like a crib. The gasoline made tinder irrelevant. He always did that part—pour on the gas and toss the match, making his red face even redder, singeing his wild beard and heavy brows. Full on crazy as fuck.

I stood up from my handiwork and waited for him to make the next move, but he just stared at me as if he'd asked me a question and was expecting the answer. "What are we sacrificing?" I asked. "We don't have anything."

He frowned his disappointment and snorted. "I had hoped that would have been revealed to you by now, but you are hard-hearted and don't listen to the Lord. *You* shall provide the sacrifice."

"I have nothing."

"You have yourself—and you belong to the Lord!"

It was finally revealed to me what was going on. I guess I should've listened to Dad's crazy fuck angels so I would know to stay off this fucking mountain. He pulled out his machete, and I grabbed a log from the top of the cradle and swung it at him. He buried his machete in it, and I grabbed both ends of

152

the log and pushed hard. He fell on his bony ass, and I doused him with gasoline, and set him off with a Zippo I'd been carrying around in my hip pocket since I was thirteen, figuring it might come in handy someday.

I ran toward the highway, looking to catch a ride into town. It was like the end of the old *Invasion of the Body Snatchers*, except I wouldn't bother to warn anybody. They'd think I was crazy anyway. All would be revealed soon enough, I reckoned. Some version or other. Repent all ye sinners! The Day of Reckoning is here! Backlit by the rising sun, a camel train wound into view, and I ran for my life.

The end of her reading is greeted with a stony silence. That's what they've come for, to diss on the phony who pretended to be a Real Writer here at the altar, the High Holy Days of Literature here in America. Come All Ye Faithful. Fair enough. Sandy never liked you guys anyway. So it's then, when she's feeling all defiant and powerful, channeling pain into strength, that she spots Daddy in the back of the auditorium, stealing out the back, his eyes downcast, apparently having heard the word that Daddy's little girl is a total fraud. *60 Minutes* cameras pan the silent crowd, zoom in on her tear-streaked-fuck-you face—material for the new headline: The Everything Girl is a Nothing Burger and a Thief.

Sandy consoles her as she packs her bags and flies away in disgrace, but it's okay—the story isn't over yet, and the rest of it is all hers. She recalls the sage advice of Jezebel, her favorite character in *Scapegoat,* "When some asshole throws you out the window, it's time to find your own room, hear what I'm saying? It's time to learn to fly."

Chapter Ten

The Trial

The Case of Della Street

Lies will flow from my lips, but there may perhaps be some truth mixed up with them; it is for you to seek out this truth and to decide whether any part of it is worth keeping.
— *Virginia Woolf, A Room of One's Own*

Even though the author photos shoot has been cancelled and the book release indefinitely postponed, Genevieve and Sandy go to the SPCA anyway to adopt a dog. The older dogs are housed up front. More difficult to adopt and usually coming from owners who have died or are too infirm to care for them any longer, they get a lot of sympathy and isn't-he/she-a-sweeties, but when it's time to adopt, most people pass them right by looking for puppies or younger dogs, wanting to delay the inevitable grief that comes from loving and losing a canine adoptee. Not Sandy. He makes a beeline for the aged dogs, and Genevieve follows. She hasn't seen him this happy since the first time they made love. It's like he's a twelve-year-old kid.

"What about this one?" he says. It's a 12-year-old black lab mix named Alice, face gone white and stiff arthritic hips, who nonetheless wags enthusiastically at the sight of them. Her former owner's in assisted living without her assistance.

"Can she see you?" Genevieve asks, surprised.

"As well as she sees anything." Her eyes are cloudy with the beginning of cataracts. "Her sense of smell's not what it used to be, so it doesn't bother her that I have no scent. She can feel me scritching her neck. She likes that."

Genevieve asks the attendant if she might visit with Alice, and she and Sandy are let inside her tiny quarters. There's a stuffed rhinoceros on the floor that looks almost as old as Alice that she scoops up and lays in Genevieve's lap, bobbing and wagging as an invitation to play. Genevieve slides the toy across the floor, and they commence a shambling game of fetch that seems to bring the ancient, ecstatically wagging dog no end of joy. Leave her in this cage, and she'll be gone in no time, Genevieve thinks. Give her a life, and she might live another 3 or 4 years of chasing Rhino and sleeping on the couch with her head in my lap. Genevieve tells the attendant, "We'll take this one."

"Are you sure? She has some health issues as you can see."

"We're all going to die," Sandy observes, "No use being in a hurry about it," and Genevieve passes on this wisdom, silencing the bright-eyed young volunteer. After a bit of paperwork and a visit to the SPCA store for a leash and collar, a few new toys, food, and treats, they're riding home in Genevieve's car, the windows rolled down, the wind in Alice's blissful face, Rhino on the seat beside her. Sandy is so delighted to have a dog in his life again, he's speechless, tears streaming down his cheeks.

How can she feel bad about resurrecting him from his long slumber, letting someone who always felt so deeply, feel again? How can she feel bad about any of it? No matter what happens. She can't wait to write about it. Sandy will be glad to lend her his name if necessary. There are bound to be more manuscripts hiding out in some real or imaginary attic somewhere. Maybe they could actually collaborate, yin and yang, the living and the dead. A dance.

Pets aren't allowed at Genevieve's tiny apartment, but fortunately she still has keys to Sandy's place, so they decide to take up residence there. Who'll notice or care? Alice, a city dog all her life, loves the great outdoors, and seems a little steadier on her feet each day, hiking up to the ridge and back, fetching sticks in the meadow.

They sit on the porch, and Sandy plays with Alice while Genevieve reads Perry Mason novels in preparation for the trial. She watched every single episode of the TV show in syndication, pretending she was Della Street and Perry Mason rolled into one with a touch of Paul Drake— who was hotter than Perry, looking a lot like Sandy, actually—but she has never read the novels. There's a shit ton on Amazon. She's addicted. Perry's one tricky customer. Roberta has secured her "a real lawyer," but Genevieve figures having Perry on her legal team can't hurt. Remembering Jennifer's request to cross-examine, Genevieve tells Roberta to leave the door open for Genevieve herself to be a cross-examiner in matters requiring literary expertise, and Roberta promises to pass that along.

Roberta's sure by now that her most famous client is as crazy as a bag of cats, but she's certainly never dull, and she likes the novels, whoever wrote them.

***

The real lawyer turns out to be Angelica Gomez, an imposing black Latina with a buzz cut in a perfectly tailored ivory suit. They meet in her Arlington office a few blocks from the National Cemetery. Sandy's gone to visit the dead so as not to overly distract Genevieve from the task at hand, claiming to have a few old friends residing there. Roberta remembers a couple of guys who died in Vietnam. John in *Death by Beauty* laments their deaths and the war without even changing their

157

names. She and Sandy plan to visit the Memorial after this meeting, tourists in DC for a day before they catch the Lynchburg train back to the Blue Ridge.

At first Angelica assumes that Genevieve wants to delay the trial as long as possible, or avoid it altogether, talking motions and countersuits and a bunch of legal gobbledygook Genevieve can scarcely track or care about. It's beside the point. It's like a chant in her head, Perry and Della and Paul chiming in: *Trial! Trial! Trial!*

"I want a jury trial. As soon as possible. The longer I'm a fraud, the longer the novels will languish—and my career as well."

Genevieve lays out her strategy, explaining that Clint mistook met-afiction for reality and told his mommy, and that's how all this nonsense got started in the first place, fueled by Tanya's greed and ambition.

Angelica gives all this a not-bad nod. "They also claim to have an expert witness, one Dr. Bent Morely who will testify that the novels are undoubtedly the work of Gene Sanders Wilkerson and that his brother Tom can corroborate this assertion. I understand that you and Morely have some history?"

"I worked for the prick. I can get a half dozen expert witnesses to say he's wrong and an incompetent to boot. No one knows more about Wilkerson than I do. I'm— I'm intimately connected to his work—of *course* he's inspired me—he's influenced every facet of my life since I was fourteen years old!" She says this last bit with disarming passion, and Angelica raises an eyebrow. "I would never in a million years, *steal* from him." *He gifted me the books—wrote them for* me. *He said so.*

"I see. No delays then?"

"The sooner the better."

"And these expert witnesses?"

"I've already sent them the novels for their professional opinions. Here are the synopses of their opinions, all signed. They are all willing to testify on my behalf."

Angelica takes the manila envelope, smiling her approval. "Is Morely so despised?"

"He's been the editor of the only Wilkerson journal around for forever and has dissed on the work of lots of touchy scholars over the years. Now they smell blood in the water. Meanwhile, I've been nice and smart and cute."

"So, which one is right—Morely or your experts?"

"Literary criticism isn't about being right."

Angelica gives that a nod. "Don't tell the jury that. We want them to believe our guys. I'm assuming they're mostly guys?"

"Four guys, two women."

"All white?"

"Afraid so."

Angelica gives that a shrug. What can you do? "The plaintiff will also claim you have a well-established history as a completely incompetent writer of fiction. They will attempt to discredit you personally."

"Bring it on."

"Sounds like you've thought about this a great deal."

"It's rather like plotting a novel."

"I suppose it is. Anything else?"

"I have a surprise witness, but I'd rather not say just yet who it is."

"A surprise witness." Angelica shakes her head with a wry smile. "Why am I not surprised?"

***

The media is even more excited by the trial than they were about The Everything Girl. *60 Minutes* hovers in the wings to see how the whole thing plays out. It's a story either way. Tom and Tanya make the talk show rounds as the wronged victim and a champion of literary authenticity and rescuer of lost children. Dr. Phil does a whole week on the psychology of the plagiarizing fraud and what it says about our sad times. Lucky for American Culture and Civilization Tanya's here to save the day.

Meanwhile Genevieve keeps her powder dry as she and Angelica put together their case. She and Sandy roam about the woods with Alice rehearsing the whole business, picnicking and making love in mountain meadows, even as the denunciations of the Everything Girl grow ever more venomous. She's a Disgrace to Literature. That's a quote. She can't believe someone said that. She loves literature, especially fiction, the art of artful lies.

The publisher, it's rumored, has two sets of title pages prepared awaiting the outcome of the trial—will they read Slidell or Wilkerson? Sandy and Genevieve know who they're rooting for. Amazon, in a bold move, accepts preorders under either name, which proves to be something of a straw poll on public opinion, which doesn't look good for Genevieve, though weirdly many people are ordering both. Meanwhile Sandy's backlist is selling like hotcakes, the proceeds, according to the ironclad stipulation of his will, going to the SPCA.

To the surprise of the plaintiffs, Genevieve gleefully accepts the motion that the proceedings be televised. Genevieve imagines herself dramatically trying on an allusive glove for the jury but can't quite work it into the plot.

***

Mom and BJ show up at the courthouse the first day while they're still empaneling a jury and proclaim their support. Mom tells her, "You were always a little strange, darling. Turns out strange works for you. If you're living in a dream, what else is new?—that's you to a T—and there ain't nothing wrong with that. This dream you got going on now is definitely your best one yet. You're going to win. I just know it." BJ bobs his head in agreement: "Give 'em hell, Sweetpea." Genevieve can scarcely believe it, but Mom's read all the novels and watches everything on TV about the case. She's not used to so much Mom attention. And all she had to do was something batshit crazy and morally reprehensible.

Genevieve sits up front at the defense table, Angelica on one side, Sandy on the other, trying to imagine what each potential juror might think of her and feels like a dog at the SPCA not knowing whether to bark or wag, shit or go blind, living a life behind bars. Angelica doesn't think there's much chance of jail should Genevieve lose this case, though criminal charges could be brought if public opinion were strong enough—to demonstrate to hapless students and aspiring writers throughout the land the steep costs of plagiarism.

During a brief recess, Genevieve tries to process the whole thing with Sandy at the end of the hall, only to have BJ walk up behind her. "Who the hell you talking to, Sweetpea?"

"I was praying," she says to test the limits of his gullibility, and he seems to buy it. He's been working on accepting a higher power in his life, a popular fiction purported to have healing powers.

Finally, the jury is empaneled. In what Angelica regards as a break for Genevieve, it's mostly women, since so many of the men pleaded their important obligations to weasel out of serving. Genevieve recalls her favorite book as a child, *The Little Engine That Could* in which the title engine was female and the other engines who told the kids to fuck off were all busy males.

After a few preliminary words from the judge, the plaintiff's lawyer, Beatty Tyborne, delivers a passionate denunciation of Genevieve and her many wicked deeds, followed by Angelica calmly tut-tutting the hysterical accusations advanced by the plaintiffs, forgiving them for they know not what they do, mistaking clever fiction for criminal fact when no crime has actually been committed, only invented.

Beatty's been on TV before, and Genevieve catches him striking a profile at key dramatic moments. He's a big barrel of a man and sways from side to side when he walks, but his suit fits him perfectly. It says: *I win a lot of cases; I make a lot of money. Fox News asks my opinion.* He calls as his first witness, Clint Cross the Betrayer who tells the tale of Genevieve's confession pretty much as it happened without too much exaggeration. It takes him quite a while to tell it all. It was a lengthy litany of thievery and deceit to get through. Not to mention her lamentations of guilt and regret. Beatty beams in triumph as he hands the witness over for cross examination.

Angelica approaches Clint, smiling. "Professor Cross, did Ms. Slidell ask you to keep what she was about to tell you in the strictest confidence, to tell absolutely no one?"

"She did."

"And you agreed to those terms, before you heard her story, pledged your utmost discretion."

"Yes."

"So how long did you keep that promise?"

"What do you mean?"

"When did you tell someone? Was it days? Weeks? Months?"

"That night."

"That very night. And whom did you tell?"

"My—my mother. Tanya Cross." He nods toward her, sitting straight and tall, proud of her only boy. One of the cameras finds her in the crowd.

"Was this immediately following Genevieve's so-called confession?"

"An hour or so later."

"And how did you spend that intervening time?"

The witness darts his eyes around the courtroom. He's never been on TV before. "I—we, Ms. Slidell and I, made love."

"And did you tell her you loved her?"

"I did."

"So, if I may summarize, Ms. Slidell tells you she has something to impart to you, which she does on the condition that you can't tell anyone, which you swear to, then after making love and pledging your love for Ms. Slidell, you call your mother to volunteer Genevieve's secrets, as if you could hardly wait. Is that a fair summary?"

"Yes." He hangs his head like the guilty dog he is.

"Did you tell your mother about the sex?"

His head snaps up, and he manages to look offended. "Certainly not."

"And where was Ms. Slidell while you were on the phone with your mother?"

"In the shower."

"It must've been a long shower."

"She takes long showers."

"I see. Was your mother the only person you told that night?"

"Yes."

"Did you tell anyone else later?"

"Yes. I told my sister, Chloe. We talk on the phone every few weeks."

"Professor Cross, your sister has a nickname for you, does she not?"

Beatty objects to this line of questioning, but the judge allows it.

"Yes, she does," Clint finally admits.

"And what is it?"

"Double Cross."

"And do you recall why she gave you that nickname?"

"When we were kids, I told Mom when Chloe did something she wasn't supposed to, broke one of the house rules. I didn't think it would matter so much, and usually it didn't. They were just stupid rules."

"And how did it 'matter so much'?"

"She and Mom had a huge fight when Chloe was fifteen, and she ran away."

"I see. And by rules, I assume you mean Mom's rules."

"Yes."

"But you thought they were stupid, wouldn't matter, so it was okay if you told on your sister, especially if it won your mother's attention and approval. Did you also promise Chloe you wouldn't tell?"

"Yes."

"On several occasions?"

"Yes."

"Fool her once, fool her twice. Shame on her, I suppose. Did you actually hear this argument?"

"I did."

"And do you precisely recall what your mother's last words were to your sister on that occasion?"

Clint's a deer in the headlights, looking desperately to poker faced Mom for guidance. Genevieve imagines a split screen of mother and son across the land.

"Would you like me to repeat the question, Professor Cross?"

"No. No. I heard you. She said, 'Get the fuck out and don't ever come back.'" There are a few gasps from the crowd. Tanya is stone-faced.

"And did she?"

"Yes."

"And how did that make you feel?"

"Awful."

"I can only imagine. So back to Genevieve. After this painful experience with your sister, why were you so quick to betray Genevieve's trust like that? Was it because you didn't actually believe her outrageous story? That it wouldn't matter because it wasn't really true? That it was just a good story. *Did* you believe her story?"

"I—I didn't know whether I totally believed it or not."

"That's the way it often is, with *fiction*, is it not, Professor?"

"But I didn't think it was fiction exactly."

"So, you totally believed it?"

"I told you, I don't *know*!"

"No further questions."

Score one for our side, Genevieve thought, but then David Philip Lancer takes the stand, the security guard she plied with pizza and coffee at 2 a.m., who she thought was more interested in checking out her ass as she fed the document feeder than in what she was doing. Turns out she was wrong.

After Beatty has Dave tell the jury what a stellar security guard he is, they get down to the night in question.

"Around 2 a.m. I was doing a building check and found Ms. Slidell working in the *Wilkerson's Studies* office."

"Were you surprised to find her there at that hour?"

"Yes, I was. Sometimes she's there late, toward the end of the semester when they have a publication deadline, but this was months before that."

"And could you describe to the jury what she was doing?"

"She was scanning a stack of pages into a laptop."

"How big was this stack?"

Dave held his hands apart, one above the other. "About yay high."

"Like this?" Beatty shows him a stack of paper and Dave says, "Exactly." Beatty then addresses the bench. "Your honor, this is exactly the number of pages in the five novel manuscripts." The judge nods; Angelica lets it pass. Exhibit A: a stack of blank pages probably abducted from the nearest Staples. "And what did Ms. Slidell do with the pages when they came out of the scanner?" Beatty asks.

"She stacked them up on the worktable beside the scanner."

"How many stacks, Mr. Lancer?"

"Five."

"And did you have occasion to return to the *Wilkerson Studies* office that night?"

"I did. At 6:45 a.m. I walked through the building, but the office door was shut. I heard a loud shrieking noise from inside that alarmed me at first, until I recognized what it was."

"And what was it, Mr. Lancer?"

"A document shredder. Sounded like it was working pretty hard."

There's a distinct muttering in the courtroom, and Genevieve can't bear to look at Sandy for fear of the distress she might see on his face. He wants her to win this case even more than she does. Genevieve's filled with the sound of the shrieking shredder in her head, and it's only Sandy's restraining hand on her shoulder that keeps her from leaping to her feet and confessing she did it. He wraps an arm around her shoulders and draws her in close. But it's not as if she *destroyed* the novels.

They're going to live forever now, one way or the other, however long forever turns out to be. The way humans are going, they might not out-live Alice.

Angelica asks Dave if he actually saw what was being shredded, and he says he didn't. Did he read any of those pages?—and he says no. But who cares? Angelica doesn't even bother to sow doubt on his shred-der ID, everyone's already got the scene riveted into their brains: That stack of pages being gobbled up in the maw of a shrieking machine, fed by a wicked harridan bent on no good, a greedy little bitch stealing from a dead man.

Next up is Bent—Professor Benton Morely—who has several bases to touch: As Genevieve's former employer and dissertation director, he depicts her as lazy, totally unreliable, even unstable, citing as evidence her abrupt (and insulting) resignation and her unprofessional text mes-sages, though the "heavy flow" line gets a few smothered smiles from the women jurors. He had never known her to work on or even mention any novels-in-progress and heard her on more than one occasion pro-claim herself to be utterly without talent as a fiction writer. His most important role, however, is to pass judgment on the novels in question as the undisputed expert on the works of Gene Sanders Wilkerson.

"Have you had the opportunity to read the novels in question, Pro-fessor Morely?"

"I have."

"In your expert opinion, would you say they could possibly be the work of Gene Sanders Wilkerson?"

"I would say there's absolutely no question." Bent launches into an extended explanation of the basis of his judgment citing syntax, im-agery, leitmotifs, objective correlatives . . . the list goes on and on, but as the juries' eyelids begin to droop, Beatty reels Bent in to double down on his thesis: These five novels are, without question, the work of none other than Gene Sanders Wilkerson, and Bent's the man who should know.

"Your witness," says Beatty.

Angelica approaches Bent with a weighty tome in hand and sets it before the witness. "Professor Morely, do you recognize this book?"

Bent preens. "I certainly do. It is my definitive annotated bibliography of the work of and scholarship pertaining to Gene Sanders Wilkerson, an indispensible contribution to the study and revival of his work. There's a companion volume of his complete surviving correspondence, thoroughly indexed and annotated."

"Quite impressive. Is there any mention of the five novels in this case to be found anywhere in either volume?"

"No."

"No mention whatsoever. No one knew they existed."

"None. No one."

"Don't you find that peculiar?"

Objection, sustained, withdraw the question, peculiar now planted in every juror's mind.

"Back to your scholarship for a moment. You say 'my' bibliography. Are these volumes entirely your work, Professor Morely. Did you have help from anyone?"

"I had *some* help, of course. It was a huge undertaking."

"More specifically, you had Ms. Slidell's help, did you not?"

"Yes."

"How long did she work with you?"

"Three years."

"Given all the work to be done, why did you continue to employ such a lazy, unreliable employee—as you described her earlier?"

"She—she is knowledgeable about Wilkerson, and enthusiastic about the subject. Not—not all the graduate students are."

"Would you say, *extremely* knowledgeable—the most knowledgeable student you've ever taught?"

"Yes. That would be a fair assessment."

"I see." Angelica taps a laptop, and a page from the Wilkerson bibliography pops up on a screen positioned so that judge, jury, and witness might take it in. "Do you recognize, this, Professor Morely?"

"I do indeed. It's a page from the Wilkerson bibliography."

"A fairly typical page?"

"I would say so. It's from the journal articles portion of the bibliography, by far the largest portion of the criticism."

"I would like you to direct your attention to the first item, 'The Quixotic Matrix of Wilkerson's *Without Regret:* The Hub As Crossroads.' I wonder if you could tell the jury a little bit about it."

"Well—the annotation is right there, and that pretty well lays it out in a nutshell I think."

"Nothing to add? It's quite complete?"

"Yes—yes, I believe so."

"There's something of an art to writing the perfect annotation, wouldn't you say?"

"I most certainly would."

"Have you *read* this particular article, Professor Morely? I remind you that you're under oath."

A fucking pop quiz. Couldn't happen to a nicer guy. "No, I don't believe I have read that particular one, actually."

"Then who wrote this flawless annotation?"

"Genevieve."

"I'm sorry, Professor Morely, could you speak a little louder so that the jury can hear you?"

"Genevieve Slidell!"

"Fair enough. She must do *something*, right? So, which of the articles on this page, did you annotate, Professor? Any one at all. Take your time."

Morely squirms and pretends to examine the page and shakes his head.

"How about this one?" A fresh page. "This one?"

Bent's head wags back and forth, as page after page fills the screen.

"Isn't it a fact that Genevieve Slidell wrote them all? Found the books and articles and letters, and so on, read them, and annotated them, each and every one?"

Bent's reply is a mere squeak, but the jury hears it loud and clear: "Yes."

"No further questions."

***

Tanya's next, to tell the story of meeting Genevieve in the wake of her son's account of her crimes. Genevieve's confiding that she was consumed with guilt is recounted in detail. Tanya feared even then that if the manuscripts actually won the contests and were published, this could be a serious legal matter and was concerned for her son. Even though Angelica gets her to admit that the optics of the case drew her in, she evades any rhetorical traps that might shake her from her story of a confession corroborating her son's account from the night before. Tanya's smooth. She might be on *The View* touting her new book, so effortless does she make it seem. Angelica manages a chuckle from the courtroom when she asks where Clint was during the confession, and Tanya says the bathroom. "This seems to be something of a family tradition."

The twins take the stand to verify that the twins in *Missing Persons* are, without question, based on them from when they were Gene Sanders Wilkerson's sisters-in-law. Angelica reads a few of the steamier passages to evoke the younger, hotter twins of the novel to mess with the jurors' ability to depict these two in their imaginations as the inspiration for much of anything except two greedy old ladies, but still they saw in the book what they saw, though as Angelica points out, we've all imagined ourselves in a novel sometime or other.

Spencer Thrush testifies to Genevieve's unqualified awfulness as a fiction writer. Beatty shows the jury his bloated vita in support of his qualifications to judge a young writer's worth.

Angelica picks apart Spencer's slender oeuvre in obscure publications and inquires if he has ever had over the years any brilliant, successful students, perhaps exceeding his paltry success, and he can't recall that he has. Angelica can, however, and reads from a letter from a fellow who almost quit writing because of Spencer's treatment of his work, but has since published a half dozen novels with Random House. "That must make you feel pretty awful," Angelica observes, letting the jury imagine all the ways it would.

Prentice was on the witness list, but Beatty decides to leave well enough alone after Spencer proved to be such a disaster. Instead, he plays his trump card, the deceased's brother, Tom Stanley Wilkerson, the plaintiff in the case.

Tom says what you'd expect him to say about his brother's talent and success and how proud he was, etc., etc., but Beatty eventually gets to the meat of the matter: "What makes you so sure these five novels are the work of your brother?"

"I'm absolutely positive. He showed them to me while he was still alive. Just a few weeks before his heart attack."

"Would you mind telling the jury about that occasion?"

"Not at all. I drove to his place to check on him. I didn't think it was too healthy to be holed up in the woods like he was, just him and his dogs, not doing a damn thing as far as I could tell except stalking through the woods like he did. He told me it was his life, and he'd do what he damn well pleased with it—which I knew was the case anyway, 'cause that's always the way he was. Couldn't tell him anything. He got especially mad when I said he wasn't doing anything, that he wasn't working. He hauls out this box of paper—manuscripts, he said—and says to me, 'You know what this is? What I've been working on all these years—five novels—like nothing I've ever done—what have you done with your life?'"

"And how many pages would you say were in this box?"

"About as many as that stack sitting over yonder." Tom points to the stack of pages fresh from their imagined shredding, as if traveling back in time to when their author still walked the earth, roamed through the woods, fought with his brother who looked a lot like Sandy if he'd lived another decade and lost his hair.

"And did you examine them?"

"I did. I looked inside, and there was a title page, like out of a book. With his name on it and all."

"And do you recall the title?"

"I do. It was *Scapegoat Phoenix*. I asked him what it meant, that it seemed like an awful peculiar title to me. Who'd want to read a book with a title like that? Can't tell what it's about."

"And what did he tell you?"

"He didn't. He just got mad and told me . . . I don't know if I should say."

"We're all adults here, Mr. Wilkerson."

"He said to fuck off."

"Did that surprise you?"

"No. He was sensitive about his work."

"So how do you suppose he'd feel about someone else taking credit for it?"

"He'd explode, I reckon. He'd hate that."

Angelica starts to object, but what's the point really?

In cross examination, she makes pretty clear that the brothers never got along, and Tom never gave a hoot about his brother's work. The profits from his other work have been shielded from the family by his will, though these five books aren't mentioned in that document. "Why do you suppose not, Mr. Wilkerson?"

"You'll have to ask him," Tom jokes, and that's that.

The plaintiff rests.

***

Angelica begins with the half dozen Wilkerson experts who bury Bent a few feet deeper with each spadeful of scorn they heap upon his work and humanity. Each goes on to pitch some theory or other showing they weren't Wilkerson's work, but most likely the work of a young woman. Beatty can never make a dent in any of their theories, while establishing that they have every reason to despise Bent. Not that it really helps their case. Let's all despise Bent, shall we? For good measure, the intern with the twin takes the stand and announces her intention to file a sexual harassment suit again the professor. Professor Emeritus chimes in with a lengthy history of Bent's crimes and a glowing assessment of Genevieve's talent and intelligence. "She did all the work and Morely took all the credit."

"Do you think it's possible she wrote these five novels?"

"I think she might accomplish anything she set her mind to."

Beatty can't lay a glove on him without looking like he's bullying a sweet old man to a jury who would all love to be his grandchild. What a sweetheart!

Bobby, Andy, and Clute take the stand to speak to Genevieve's professionalism that persuaded them all that she was the author she claimed to be. Angelica asks Clute to address the issue of metafiction. The jury seems rapt if a bit dazed, and then he goes off on a riff about attics, how the novels are like the mad wife in *Jane Eyre*, locked away from the world by an all but dead white man, and how they are the perfect objective correlative to embody the long shackled female imagination Virginia Woolf laments in *A Room of One's Own*. Genevieve has imaginatively set them free in a unique triumph of the imagination characteristic of the finest fantastika. Beatty's no match for Clute, and, though the jury's not a hundred percent sure what he said, he certainly was impressive.

The editor of the five novels takes the stand and explains that the novels as they are about to be published are significantly different from the originally submitted manuscripts. She explains the editorial process to the jury, how the editor endeavors to suggest improvements that will make it a better book.

"So, you suggest changes, and the writer then makes them?"

"It's not so simple. Some things are minor, but some are quite substantive, the reimagining of a secondary character, for example."

"And to whom did you suggest these changes?"

"To Ms. Slidell."

"So, what did she do with your suggestions?"

"She soared with him. She rejected some, of course—all authors do—and persuaded me her way was better, and on other quite complex issues, she outdid my expectations by a good measure."

"So, it is your belief that she was the author?"

"Absolutely."

"And why were you chosen to be her editor?"

"Because I have experience in a wide range of genres, I imagine."

"And what do you make of Ms. Slidell pursuing so many different genres all at once?"

"I find it delightful."

***

Seems like a good time to call Genevieve to the stand.

Angelica has her recount the story of her long association with and passion for the work of Gene Sanders Wilkerson, her labors in the vineyards of scholarship, and her eventual turning to fiction in an ambitious project she called *The Perfect Stranger*, quoting the Wilkerson passage to the jury.

"Would you mind telling the jury how this project came to be, and how it has evolved?"

"I'd be glad to. While I was working in the Wilkerson cabin these last few years with hours alone in the place, I had the idea of someone like me finding these old undiscovered manuscripts, and then I started thinking about why they were undiscovered and decided that they must be weird in some way, so that their creator might doubt them. Literarily spooky—like a mainstream guy like Wilkerson suddenly going full-tilt genre—genres, which is even weirder—and that gave me the incept for the story. Famous dead author v. the literary world."

"Incept? What is that?"

"It's what we novelists call the germ of an idea, the flash of insight that gives birth to what follows."

"I see. And what did you do with this germ of a story?"

175

"I came up with five wacky premises and handed them over to the Sandy who has haunted my imagination since I was a girl, and let him play. He needed play. He was a lonely old man who'd lost the love of his life. He was delighted to help me. Once the ghost showed up in the story, I figured I might have a movie, and I started thinking of it in those terms. How do the four novels make a whole? Five, actually. Even though *The Mad Statue* doesn't win anything. It's essential to the conceit. It's the work the author loves best of all even though the world refuses to validate it."

"And then what did you do?"

"I wrote them."

"All five novels?"

"Yes."

"Was that entirely necessary to the project?"

"I suppose not, but they proved an indispensible part of the process. By channeling Wilkerson with all I know about his life and work, the larger story of which they're a part evolved organically, a symbiotic relationship.

"Personally, it all comes out of my sense of Unworthiness to be a Real Writer. The stories are all the same story—the longing to get your story told and heard. To become real and authentic in some way or other, even when your whole life is a fiction."

"When you entered the novels in all those contests, did you think they would actually win?"

"Not really. I wanted to have that experience of putting myself out there, so I could write about it."

"And what if you had lost? Isn't their winning essential to the larger story?"

"Not really. I would've *pretended* that they had. It's all a story, all make believe. Only in this, case parts of it became real."

"I see."

"And how is the larger story doing?"

"It's almost done. I just need to write the trial and the HEA, happily ever after. I then plan to adapt it into a screenplay myself. I've always wanted to write one of those."

"As did Wilkerson, I believe?"

"Definitely. He regretted never adapting his own work when he was alive."

"Do you have a partner in this venture?"

"Two. Sandy Wilkerson's ghost who guides my every word." Genevieve stares lovingly at Sandy sitting in his chair at the defense desk.

"You mean metaphorically."

"Of course." *My little metaphoric pumpkin.*

"You said two?"

"Jennifer Lawrence."

"The famous actress?"

"Yes."

The courtroom goes nuts for a few minutes while the judge gavels for silence.

Genevieve explains that when she first decided to tell the story in a screenplay, she pitched the idea to Jennifer Lawrence who has been unbelievably supportive throughout the entire process.

She's standing by on Skype, Angelica says, if the court will allow.

Who's going to say no to Jennifer Lawrence? Her face fills the screen, and she totally charms the jury with her ringing endorsement of Genevieve Slidell and her brilliant screenplay she looks forward to bringing to life on the big screen.

Beatty slumps in his chair like a deflated balloon. The *60 Minutes* folks are trading high fives, and Sandy's dancing on the table like a dervish. Tanya tries to look stoic, and Tom doesn't know what hit him.

"No questions," Beatty says, and the defense rests.

In his closing argument, Beatty tries to persuade with the only thing left of his case—that stack of papers that Tom swears his brother wrote, but it's boiled down to his word against Genevieve's, with Genevieve's version of the truth destined to be the next Jennifer Lawrence movie, and Tom's Another Old White Guy Wins Again.

Who would you vote for? Not you exactly. You know too much, are intimate with the perfect stranger. You might vote any which way. But those trapped inside the story, shielded from the business of creation, they haven't any such illusion of freedom.

The jury takes twenty minutes to decide in Genevieve's favor.

Afterwards, Jennifer's a little disappointed that her character doesn't get to cross-examine anyone, but Angelica nixed the idea and doubted the judge would go for it. Genevieve consoles Jennifer by pointing out that the final screenplay might still give her the chance—it's a movie, after all, not reality. "At least I get to testify," Jennifer observes philosophically. "I wouldn't want to just sit there without sticking up for myself. You did great, by the way. I'm going to have fun being you."

Chapter Eleven

Happily Ever After

The Mother and Child Reunion

"A woman must have money and a room of her own if she is to write fiction."

— Virginia Woolf, A Room of One's Own

Trevor Hatchette makes a surprise pilgrimage to the cabin to inform Genevieve he's dropping his lawsuit now that he's finally read her novel and watched her trial on TV—seems he was one of those who preordered both authors. "It made me laugh. It was nothing like my book. Somebody thought it would be fun to set me off. Sorry. Is it going to be an HBO series? Netflix?"

"Maybe eventually. They've bid themselves up so high it will have to make *Game of Thrones* look like a flop sitcom to make any money." It's hard to care. She has plenty of money and can write whatever the hell she wants. Sandy points out that no series means she won't have a flop to live down, even if she had nothing to do with it unless she wrote it herself, which she has no intention of doing. Writing a series sounds like a sentence, not an opportunity. She wants to try new stuff. *60 Minutes* talks to Trevor as an SF icon, and he sings her praises and says he discovered her. "Besides," he says, "I wouldn't want that prick

Wilkerson to get all the credit. And the little brother's an even bigger prick."

This seems to please Sandy no end, which surprises her at first, until she thinks about it. An enduring feud makes him feel more alive. That's the thing about Sandy—the more he acts like he's alive, the more he is. Every day he's a little bit warmer. Or perhaps she's a little more mad. What happens when the mad woman in the attic climbs down into a room of her own? Plus, twenty acres of woods, a creek running through the heart of it that sings to her all night through the bedroom window, except in winter when it freezes up, and everything is snow-covered and still. She loves it up here.

Anderson Cooper finally has his interview at the cabin where Genevieve plans to reside as the director of the Wilkerson Foundation she's establishing in cooperation with the University. She will also be editing the American Library Edition of Wilkerson's novels with her reworked dissertation serving as introduction. As well as finishing *The Perfect Stranger*—which is how the whole thing began, and the five novels came to be. Genevieve recites this exposition to Anderson for those late to the party as they wander through the woods with the camera lovingly taking in the riot of vegetation and wildlife of spring in the Blue Ridge, and Genevieve's terrified the camera man's going to trip over a root and break her neck, but she's as sure footed as a goat walking uphill and backwards.

Later, they're lounging on the porch at dusk almost drowned out by crickets and cicadas, and the sound man's having a cow trying to get a level on Genevieve, and she can't quit laughing. They're having rum toddies, and the hairdresser, who just shot a story in Denver gave her a happy little after dinner mint if she was so inclined. They're all getting tired of this great outdoors thing, except Genevieve who knows what comes next. The sunset barely gets a shrug. It's not a mountain valley's best move; the sun lingers too long beyond the ridge. But even Anderson gets wide-eyed when the lightning bugs come out, and they're nothing compared to the stars—billions and billions—and starry-eyed Anderson lets her babble whatever comes into her head in the half-light through the cabin windows—about writing, about the screenplay, about Sandy, about Jennifer, who can't make it in person because she's filming in the Arctic for the next six months. The plan is to start shooting *Perfect Stranger* when she's had a chance to thaw out.

Sandy perches on the porch rail and takes it all in, mostly pleased, with a touch of jealousy. *You do know the man's gay, don't you?*

Of course she knows. Anderson's her type when she can find him, someone like Sandy. She mouths "later" to her ghost lover and keeps on flirting.

"What else are you working on?" Anderson asks. "Have you abandoned the novel?"

"Oh my, no. Don't say it like that. You make me feel like some mother in a murder ballad who murders her babies." She makes Anderson laugh. He has sparkly eyes. "I love the novel," she says. "I'll be back. I'm in the process of revising *The Mad Statue.*"

"The Forgotten Novel," Anderson says, "as it's come to be known."

Genevieve laughs and downs her toddy. "We'll just have to see if I can change that."

He asks a few follow-up questions, but she says she prefers not to discuss work in progress, blah, blah, blah, so they edit all that out.

"Anything else coming out soon?" Anderson asks

"I have a short story in *The New Yorker* next month."

"Isn't this a story you wrote in Spencer Thrush's workshop?"

"It is."

They show a clip from Thrush's testimony at the trial. "And how does that make you feel?" Anderson inquires.

"Spencer's okay. He was just trying to do his job as he saw it. I did revise the story on Sandy's recommendation, and that made all the difference. It wasn't the same sucky story Spencer read."

"Sandy? You mean Gene Sanders Wilkerson."

"Yes. The one and only. A life-long obsession. We collaborate on everything."

Anderson smiles at her sweetly. *Isn't she something! She seems to actually believe this stuff! How charming!*

Anderson would definitely be her type if he wasn't gay. Not that she's looking. She found the love of her life a long time ago.

"Is it lonely?" Anderson asks.

And she replies, "Writing's always lonely." She and Sandy go out in the world on occasion, but she has to disguise her appearance and they scarcely get a moment alone. Here they get to be themselves.

"When I get crazy lonely, I drive into Lynchburg and catch a matinee, so I won't have to drive back on the winding roads at night. It doesn't much matter what the movie is as long as it carries me along into another world, not that I'm not delighted with the one I'm living in—my wildest dreams come true. Sometimes it's cold at night, but Sandy keeps me warm."

Anderson loves that. Is it telling when no one believes you? Sandy beams his pleasure, so he's almost one of those silly glowing movie ghosts, and the thought makes Genevieve laugh out loud.

***

It takes all night for the *60 Minutes* crew to pack up and leave. Gone are the rumbling generators, the scaffolding, the lights, the smell of food Genevieve wouldn't eat if her life depended on it. Sandy, a vegetarian ever since his third marriage, soon persuaded Genevieve it was good for her and the planet not to eat other beasts. She grows a lot of their food, is learning how to cook. Sandy's correspondence is full of recipes. He loved to cook and still does.

Now that all her wildest dreams have come true, the pressure's on to make new ones. Who wants to live their life without wildest dreams? Not Genevieve certainly. For now, she's enjoying writing the screenplay. Sandy never gives her ideas—it's her story, he insists—but she bounces hers off him until it's hard to say exactly whose idea it ends up being—doesn't matter, if it works. She's launched into it, and he's not her *guia*—she had her fill of those in Ocosingo. He's a trusted friend, the perfect stranger, who helps her figure out where they're going and what it all might mean, if anything. Since neither of them has ever written a screenplay, they figured a detailed outline would be a good idea.

Their work habits are different. She likes to stagger out of a deep sleep and wild dreams before dawn, pour coffee, and wake up the laptop. Sandy likes ritual. He runs with Alice, does some yoga and meditation, brews a pot of aromatic tea, and lights a stick of incense about the time she's finished that first cup, and they'll talk about what she's working on, the moments of the story as they unfold.

Today is a big day. They've finished another draft of *The Mad Statue*, though it's still not quite right, so they're going to give it a rest for a while and launch into the screenplay. They've made a lovely outline. She can see every scene in her head. Now all she has to do is put it on a screen, on a page, on a multitude of screens into untold strangers' lives.

Alice died last week, and they wept and wailed, and buried her in the meadow. Her ghost showed up a few days later, curled up at their feet as they write. When it's getting really good, she starts dreaming, her paws twitching, emitting chirpy muted barks of great intensity. A ground hog. A wild turkey. A new life.

They begin:

THE PERFECT STRANGER

Written by
Genevieve Slidell

EXT. WILKERSON CABIN - DAY (FALL)

A rustic cabin situated in a Blue Ridge mountain valley meadow, a BABBLING creek running along-side. The meadow is surrounded by woods teeming with wildlife—crows CAWING, WIND in the trees.

A SERIES OF SHOTS - MOUNTAIN LIFE

A) A GROUNDHOG WADDLES UP A TRAIL

B) A CRAYFISH SCUTTLES BENEATH THE RUSHING WATER

C) A BLACK SNAKE SLITHERS THROUGH HIGH GRASS

D) A WATCHFUL HAWK SPOTS PREY BELOW AND TAKES FLIGHT

INT. WILKERSON CABIN/LIVING ROOM - DAY

The interior is filled with memorabilia and de-tritus of the successful writing career of GENE SANDERS WILKERSON — awards, framed book jackets, photos with celebrities, computer and paraphernalia circa 1999, photos with exes and dogs.

GENEVIEVE O.S.
Sound of her THUMPING about the Attic.

INT. WILKERSON CABIN/ATTIC

Cramped and full of junk layered in dust.

GENEVIEVE

Wearing a headlamp and facemask, navigating through the dust and junk, she is filthy, BREATHING HEAVILY.

Fuck, Fuck, Fuck.

Her lamp finds a BOX in the corner. She makes her way to the box, crawling to reach it, and drags it to the Attic opening. The lid is labeled with acronyms — TMS, SPH, SSD.

Holy shit! Should I, or shouldn't I?
Stupid question.

She peels off the packing tape and removes the lid and shines her light inside the box to reveal the SCAPEGOAT PHOENIX TITLE PAGE.

Coming Soon!

Leaving the Dead

Leaving the Dead is a collection of fifteen stories about the long slow dance with death and the heartbreak of life…

•When a writer runs into the ghost of his father who died of Alzheimer's, death has restored his memory, and he's eager to share.

•An unlikely couple and an abandoned seeing eye dog find happiness after everyone else dies.

•A college freshman goes home for the holidays with her lover who claims to be a robot—and takes her to an abandoned factory on Christmas Eve where she was born.

And more!

by
DENNIS DANVERS
author of *Circuit of Heaven*
End of Days, and *The Fourth World*

For more information
visit: www.SpeakingVolumes.us

Coming Soon!

The Soothsayer & the Changeling

Thus begins, *The Soothsayer & the Changeling* in which the varied self-absorbed lives of a stunning beauty, a no-talent screenwriter, a bereaved Christian widow, a disgraced professor, an over-medicated depressive, and a lonely mountain boy with a way with animals are woven together to yield a dream of doom to awaken the slumbering world before it's too late.

Promising epiphany over apocalypse, *The Soothsayer & the Changeling* pits our deeply personal obsessive lives against a dying planet upon which all our dreams depend, and offers the possibility of hope and love.

by
DENNIS DANVERS
author of *Circuit of Heaven*
End of Days, and *The Fourth World*

For more information
visit: www.SpeakingVolumes.us

On Sale Now!

**For more information
visit:** www.SpeakingVolumes.us

On Sale Now!

THE
RED SHOELACE
KILLER

A MINNIE MARKWOOD MYSTERY

S U S A N   S U N D W A L L

Published by SpeakingVolumes

For more information
visit: www.SpeakingVolumes.us

On Sale Now!

www.ingramcontent.com/pod-product-compliance
Lightning Source LLC
Chambersburg PA
CBHW020606250626
47154CB00004B/1378